FLAWLESS

SELENA BAILEY BOOK 5

H.K. CHRISTIE

KEEKSTAR
MEDIA

First edition: January 2022

ISBN: 978-1-953268-09-9

1

STEPHANIE, AGE 25

HEART POUNDING IN MY EARS, I LEANED AGAINST THE countertop as I entered the day's run into my fitness app. Despite some queasiness and my spinning head, I had never felt better, and I couldn't believe I had run the entire sixty minutes - no stopping. Sweat dripped onto my linoleum floor like a light rain - I had done well. The other women I'd met at the clinic told me how exercise could really help with slimming down fast. Some of them ran for two hours a day. I wasn't there yet, but I was working up to it. Running made me feel strong. Maybe not physically in that moment but at least mentally. I was taking control of my life. I had never been thinner than I was right now. No more fat jokes. No more squeezing into clothes. No more squishy belly.

I pushed off the counter, walked into my living room, and plopped myself down onto my new yoga mat. Still slightly out of breath, I stretched out my overworked muscles as I replayed today's wins through my mind.

He came by my desk again. Thankfully, I had been sitting down, since those gray-blue eyes and wide smile made me weak in the knees. When he spoke to me, it was like we were the only two people in the room. As if we were in our own little bubble. He hadn't asked me out yet, but I felt like he actually might. The way he looked at me so intently it was as if he were studying my whole being. There was something about him that made me want to scream, 'be with me.' He was tall and lean, and he needed someone who was his physical match. I wasn't as tall and never would be, but I would be thin. I was proud of myself that I had lost thirty pounds in the last month and a half. He had never spoken to me before I started losing weight, but over the past two weeks, he'd stopped by my desk every day. I swore that going to the clinic had changed my life. I was finally going to be the perfect size, have the perfect guy, the perfect job, and my life would finally be as it was supposed to be.

I glanced at my phone and realized I only had forty-five minutes before my sister was going to be at my apartment to pick me up for happy hour and shopping. For the first time, or at least in my memory, I was excited to go clothes shopping. I was no longer double digits. I was a size six. *Six.* I loved how that sounded. I was smaller than I was when I was ten years old.

I had to look my best in order to get him to ask me out and for us to become a couple. Two fit, thin, attractive people - it would be worth it. It was different this time - I could feel it. I hadn't eaten an entire package of Oreos in over a month. *Mmm. Oreos.* No, I wouldn't have any cookies, especially since there were none in my apartment. I'd replaced my previous snacks of cookies and ice cream, chips and soda with healthy plain yogurt and fruit. If this was what it took to be thin - I was all in. I didn't know what those vitamins the doctor had given me were, but if you asked me, I'd say they were tiny miracles. That woman I had met was obviously wrong - they were perfectly safe and highly effective.

After I finished stretching, I climbed to my feet and reached for the couch to steady myself. The room was spinning. My heart beat faster and faster - almost out of control. Maybe I had overdone it at the gym and hadn't eaten enough today. I had been saving my calories to go out to dinner with Vicki. *I'll have a banana. That always helps with the dizzies.* My sister couldn't know how much I had been restricting my calories, and to keep up that ruse, I would have to eat an entire meal and have a cocktail. She didn't approve of 'fad' dieting and had insisted I'd lost too much weight, too fast. But I think Vicki had never approved of my weight loss plans because she didn't understand what it was like. She had always been thin and beautiful and successful. I had always been the chubby, or worse, 'big boned', younger sister. Not anymore.

After a deep breath, I went into the kitchen and grabbed a banana from the rack. Peeling it as fast as I could, I munched it down. The sweetness filled my body, which relaxed ever so slightly. I finished chewing and headed toward the bathroom where I stripped off my spandex and contorted out of my sports bra, throwing the sweaty clothes onto the ground before I stared down at my nemesis, my monster - the villain I would defeat.

My scale.

With my eyes shut, I stepped atop it. It was time for the moment of truth. I had been really good this week and hadn't weighed myself yet. Eyes open, I read the digital numbers and grinned. I was down two more pounds - only six pounds from my goal weight. I glanced up in the mirror and frowned. Pinching my thighs, I contemplated whether my goal weight was low enough. There was flab on my thighs and my arms. I still had fat. I hated fat. Shaking my head in disgust, I reached over the tub to turn on the water. The room spun. I clutched my chest as I crumpled to the floor, banging my head on the sink on the way down. Gasping, I saw stars and then darkness.

2

SELENA

DASHING THROUGH THE PARKING LOT, I MADE IT TO THE entrance to my office with three minutes to spare. My first client, Vicki Crawford, would arrive in mere moments to discuss her sister's case. I'd spent so much time picking out the right outfit and the right accessories that I had lost track of time. It wouldn't happen again. I fiddled with the keys before I unlocked the door but paused and then stepped back to admire the signage.

Bailey Investigations.

I didn't think I would ever tire of seeing my company name on the outside of my office. At twenty-one years old, I was a licensed private investigator, mostly thanks to my stepmother Martina, who let me work at her firm for the last few years so I could get enough hours to even qualify for it. Not only that, but I also had my own office and brand new business cards along with a real investigation, not just a simple background check. I pushed open the door to my two hundred square-foot office and grinned. It was tiny, but it was all mine.

I flipped on the lights and walked over to the desk, setting down my backpack next to the chair. Seated, I pulled a compact mirror from the front pocket and studied my reflection. Thankfully, I hadn't run so much that I'd sweated. After reapplying my lip gloss, I brushed my hair out of my face. It was time. Slipping the compact back into my backpack, I sat up straight and powered up my computer.

Glancing at the time in the monitor's corner, I saw that I had one minute before Vicki was supposed to arrive for her appointment. We had spoken on the phone the day before when she explained she needed help to figure out what was happening to her sister, who lay quietly in the intensive care unit at the local hospital. I was driven by the thrill of the investigation, but I also wanted to make sure Vicki's sister, Stephanie, didn't die before I could help her - if I could help her. No. Not could. I would help her. It was what I did. It was in my bones. It was who I was. I was Selena Bailey, private investigator.

I opened my email application to read emails. With minor disappointment, I realized I didn't have very many. My lips curled up in a smile as I saw one from Martina. I clicked open the email with the subject line: *Good luck today.*

Hi Selena,

Good luck today! I know you have your first big meeting with your client. I know you'll do great. Let me know if you want to talk or if you need anything.

Love,

Martina

It went without saying that I had won the stepmother lottery. Over the last four years, Martina had saved me, guided me, taught me, and helped me become the person I was. If only I could be half as good as she was at private investigations, I would do all right.

Suddenly, I was sent back to the first time I had met Martina. She had stormed into the cabin where I was being held hostage. I was on the ground while my psycho boyfriend straddled me with a gun to my head. Martina shot him, and he fell to the side. When I'd scrambled up from the floor, I had looked up at this woman - this warrior. Her amber eyes met mine. She lowered her weapon and asked, "Are you okay?"

Was I okay? I had been held hostage by my boyfriend, who was planning to kill me. But for some reason, at that moment, in Martina's presence, I had felt okay. From that moment forward, my life changed. I was only seventeen years old, and my mother had been killed a few months earlier. Unbeknownst to me, at the time, both my father and Martina were looking for me. With Martina's investigative skills and connections, she had hooked up with the local police department in the search. They found me just in the nick of time.

Until the day I had met her, and she reunited me with my father, I thought I was an orphan. But now I had the most loving family I could ever imagine. I stilled missed my mom, but it was nice to have my dad, Martina, and my stepsister, Zoey. Zoey was definitely my opposite, but it made our holidays and family gatherings even more fun. Zoey was outgoing and loved people and places and shiny objects. I was a bit more like Martina, with my black wardrobe and more introverted nature. But I was my father's daughter. He was quiet and reserved, as was I. Martina could be all up in your face when she felt it was necessary. She was fierce.

I was one lucky twenty-one-year-old college grad with a loving family and her own business. At times, I couldn't believe this was my life. The last four years had been turbulent, with so many ups and so many downs - so very far down.

That was over. It had to be. It was all up from here.

A gush of wind from the opening of my office door drew my attention toward the entrance of my office. A woman, dressed in skinny jeans and a white turtleneck sweater with dark, flowing hair, walked in. I collapsed my email, stood up, and walked around my desk to greet her. "Are you Vicki Crawford?"

"Yes."

I extended my hand. "I'm Selena. It's nice to meet you in person."

"Likewise," she said with an apprehensive smile.

I didn't take her reserved attitude personally. She was going through her own version of hell. From what I understood, she and her sister, Stephanie, were best friends. Stephanie was lying unconscious in the intensive care unit, and the doctors didn't know if they could save her. I offered her the chair across from my desk. "Would you like some coffee or anything? Maybe water or tea?"

Hopefully, that's all she wanted. I had a Keurig for coffee or tea and bottled water in the fridge. That was it. I'd only been in business for two days and was living on my savings.

Vicki said, "I'm fine, thank you."

"How is Stephanie doing?" I asked.

"The doctors say she's stable but that it could go in any direction. If we can find out what she has taken - assuming she has - they said it could help."

"And the police won't help at all?" I asked.

"They said there's been no foul play. They didn't find anything in her apartment that looked suspicious."

I would be the judge of that. "Well, let's see if we can get to the bottom of this, and fast."

Vicki nodded. "That would be great."

"When we spoke on the phone, you said Stephanie had recently started seeing a weight loss doctor, and he gave her vitamins, which led to a large amount of weight loss in the last month or two?"

"That's right. I don't know the doctor's name. She told me she started going to some clinic and that they were helping her lose weight and get healthy. She said they were just vitamins and that it was the support at the clinic that helped her stick to her diet. The doctor said it was important to take the vitamins because with a lot of weight loss, you can lose minerals and other vital nutrients because of the decrease in food intake. She swore they were vitamins and not a drug but—" She gripped her purse and gritted her teeth.

"But you don't believe that?" I asked.

"I don't. Stephanie wasn't a large woman to begin with. She'd always been obsessed with her weight over the years. As far back as I can remember. But she's never been big or obese or someone who you would look at and say they needed to go on a diet. I had insisted she didn't need to diet and that she was beautiful, but she didn't listen. But then she lost so much weight. She's dropped about thirty pounds in less than two months. When I saw her last, her clothes were practically falling off her, and I could see her collarbones."

That seemed suspicious. I wondered if I had ever looked at someone and thought they should go on a diet. Had I ever been that judgmental? Did people judge me? I ate fairly healthy, especially for a twenty-one-year-old, and I worked out at least five days a week. I had never been really obsessed with my weight or my appearance, not really. But maybe I had but hadn't realized it? "Do you know how she found out about this weight loss doctor?"

"From a coworker. Apparently, they'd started a weight loss challenge at work, and Stephanie wanted to win. She said she wanted to fit into her 'goal weight' jeans."

I couldn't imagine buying clothes that didn't fit at the time of purchase. But I supposed it would be a motivator if you had a weight loss goal. Then again, it was like buying the prize before winning the competition. Wouldn't it make more sense to hit your goal weight and then pick something out that made you feel good?

"Do you have this coworker's name?"

"I have a first name and the name of her company. I can provide all of that to you."

"Perfect."

Vicki pulled a notepad out of her purse, ripped off the top piece and slid it across the desk to me. I read the note that contained Stephanie's coworker's name, the address for her workplace, and her home address. Vicki had come prepared.

"Do you know how much Stephanie weighed before she went to the weight loss doctor?"

"I don't know. She never would talk about her weight. She's really sensitive about it. But I just have to think this doctor isn't on the up and up. Stephanie wasn't somebody who seemed large enough to need to go to a weight loss clinic or a doctor or get any kind of medication for it. She was just average size."

The fashion industry reported that in the U.S., the average women's dress size was between a size 16 and 18. Yet, most models were a size 0. Maybe Stephanie was trying to achieve a much thinner look like you'd find on social media or in the movies? Maybe she was searching for what she considered perfection?

"Do you remember when Stephanie began having concerns about her weight?"

Vicki let out a breath. "As far back as I can remember. Probably from back when she was a preteen or early teens. I don't know, maybe twelve or thirteen."

Yikes. I certainly wasn't thinking about dieting when I was thirteen. Or when I was eighteen. I hadn't even considered my diet or exercise routine until I'd met Martina. She had told me to have a strong mind, I needed to have a strong body too, which meant eating healthy and regular exercise. She had never commented on my looks are even said that I had a poor diet or needed to lose weight. Just that it was important to be healthy. I wasn't totally naïve. Living in the college dorms, I knew there were a lot of women with eating disorders - especially living on our floor. One time, I had walked into the common bathroom and heard someone throwing up and offered her help. I thought she had been sick. She flushed the toilet and exited the stall. She waved me off and said it was how she stayed thin. I thought that was crazy. But I soon found she wasn't exactly a needle in a haystack. She wasn't the minority. Most women I'd met in college worried about their size. Counting calories. Looking good for men. Until I'd received the call from Vicki and did some research on eating disorders, I had assumed that behavior was normal. Why was that normal? It shouldn't be normal.

"What else can you tell me about Stephanie?"

Vicki pulled the folder out of her purse. She flipped it open and passed me a photograph. Vicki was *very* prepared.

The photo was of a woman with the same dark hair as Vicki, with a wide smile and sparkling blue eyes. She was beautiful, by conventional standards and really anybody's standards.

"That's Stephanie. She's beautiful. I never understood why she was so obsessed with her weight. Anyhow, she's not just beautiful, she's smart. She's twenty-five years old. She graduated from college with a degree in communications and works in HR. She's good at her job, and she's smart with her money. She has lots of friends. She's funny and caring, and she's my best friend..." Vicki bowed her head and cried.

I grabbed the box of tissues on my desk and set it down in front of Vicki. I hadn't thought I needed the tissues for my office, but Martina had insisted that I did. Martina was almost always right. At times, it was annoying, and other times, it was useful knowing she would always have the answer.

Vicki calmed and dried her eyes. "I'm sorry. It's so hard to believe that she could die."

I said, "We'll make sure that doesn't happen," with more confidence than I actually had. "Was Stephanie in a relationship?"

"No. She's had a few over the years, but nothing recent. She thought losing weight was going to get her a boyfriend. I always told her she was beautiful and didn't need to lose any weight and any guy would be happy and lucky to have her. She didn't agree."

"Stephanie sounds like an amazing woman. I will figure out what was going on at the doctor's office and get you as much information as I can to make sure she gets better."

"I appreciate that. What do we do next?" Vicki asked.

"Well, as I said on the phone yesterday, I'd like to visit her apartment, so if you have the key, I can look around and see if I can find any medications she may have taken that the police didn't find. After that, I'll question her coworker to see if I can get the name of that doctor, and then I'll pay him a visit."

Vicki nodded.

"I have a few other clients, but you're my top priority. I'll get started right away. Do you want to go with me to her apartment, or would you prefer I go alone?"

"I have to get back to the hospital. I want to be there if she wakes up."

"I think that's a great idea. You should be with Stephanie." I actually preferred searching the apartment on my own. Who knew what I'd find at Stephanie's apartment? If she had anything embarrassing or something she didn't want her sister to see, I would want to respect that.

"Thank you, Selena. If you get any information, you'll call me right away? You have my cell phone number, right?"

"Of course."

Vicki Crawford gave me the key to her sister's apartment along with the notes she had about Stephanie's employer's address and her photograph. It wasn't a lot to go on, but hopefully it would be enough to figure out what happened to Stephanie and why. We said our goodbyes, and I watched as she exited the office out to the parking lot. I returned to my desk and did a quick glance at my email before packing up my backpack with everything I would need for the day. Zipped and ready to go, I slipped a strap over my shoulder and set out to search for answers.

3

SELENA

Wearing latex gloves, I unlocked the front door to Stephanie Crawford's apartment. I wasn't entering a crime scene as far as I knew, but I wanted to take precautions in the event I found something we'd need to check for trace evidence. The gloves would ensure I didn't leave any of my own fingerprints throughout the apartment. Before pushing the door open, I glanced back at the surrounding apartments. There were no other people out. *Thank goodness. I look like a burglar and really don't need any police interference.* Next time, I'd wear something other than a black sweater and black jeans with black boots. I entered the apartment and carefully shut the door behind me.

Inside, I checked out the small apartment. There was a kitchen and living room visible from the entry. I presumed the bedroom and bathroom were to the left. *Might as well start with the kitchen.* Opening up each cupboard, I found dishes, cups, and an assortment of mismatched mugs. There was nothing terribly out of the ordinary and, more importantly, no pills. I turned to the other side of the small kitchen and studied the refrigerator door. Attached with magnets were photographs of

Stephanie and her sister and several others of Stephanie with, presumably, her friends, based on their age and youthful smiles. They all looked happy. Stephanie looked happy.

Popping open the fridge, I surveyed the contents. It was clear Stephanie was a fan of healthy eating. All she had was a bag of apples, broccoli, and plain yogurt with a few assorted condiments. My guess was Stephanie didn't cook much.

I opened up the freezer. *A-ha.* Stacks of frozen meals filled the space, and I guessed frozen diet meals were the majority of what Stephanie ate. Reading the meal descriptions, I found nothing from a special diet program but more likely all commonly found at the grocery store. She seemed partial to the meatloaf with mashed potatoes. No ice cream or dessert of any kind that I could see.

Being a healthy eater myself, I understood having fruits and veggies, but I also had a stash of cookies and even the occasional pint of ice cream in my freezer. Then again, I also wasn't a life-long dieter and hadn't ever been too concerned over my weight. Was that even true? Maybe it wasn't. I recalled when I had fallen off the gym wagon for a while, and my clothes had gotten a little snug. I certainly hadn't liked that. But I hadn't counted calories or joined a weight loss program. I simply got my butt back in the gym again. I know, for a lot of women, exercise alone wasn't enough to slim down. If the gym hadn't been enough for me, would I have turned to counting calories?

I shut the freezer and looked through the cupboards on the other side of the kitchen. Nothing interesting inside.

I exited the kitchen and turned around, admiring how clean it was. There were no dishes in the sink or scuffs on the floor or crumbs on the counter.

Continuing in the living room, I thought it was cool. I liked Stephanie's style. There was a matching gray sofa and loveseat and a television in the center of the living room. Abstract art adorned the walls. I walked toward the TV console and studied the collection of DVDs and books on the shelf. They were mostly various exercise boot camps and workouts, with a collection of thriller novels.

Leaned up against the wall, next to the TV, were a yoga mat and a few free weights.

In the dining area, there was a small table and chairs in the corner with a bouquet of flowers in the middle. I inspected the colorful blooms closer. They looked like they came from the grocery store, not likely something that was a delivery or gift. Or maybe they were. Vicki said Stephanie didn't have a boyfriend, but maybe she didn't know everything about her sister.

Then again, maybe Stephanie bought the flowers for herself. Like her sister had said, she was smart, funny, and the life of the party. Her apartment was stylish and clean. She had nice things. Why not buy some flowers to brighten up the room?

Should I buy flowers to brighten up my room? Not sure it was possible. I rented a room that only included a spot for my bed, a closet, a kitchenette, and a bathroom. Maybe after I got a paycheck or two, I would consider upgrading.

Continuing down the hallway, I reached a bedroom on the right and a rather large bathroom on the left. *I could certainly get used to a place like this.*

I turned into the bathroom and spotted a scale on the floor. This was where she'd fallen and collapsed - where Vicki had found her.

Over the sink was a mirrored medicine cabinet. I crossed my fingers, hoping I'd find something there. Inside, I found facial cleanser, moisturizer, sunscreen, a round plastic disc of birth control pills, and vitamins - a lot of vitamins: B12, vitamin C, vitamin D, and a multivitamin.

Did she have a boyfriend? Inconclusive. The contraceptives weren't that big of a surprise. After all, women didn't only take a contraceptive to prevent pregnancy. Some took it to regulate their hormones to help with acne, cramps, headaches, and to reduce PMS symptoms. Certainly couldn't make an assumption because she was on the pill.

Disappointed, I shut the cabinet. I hadn't found any mysterious pills from the equally mysterious weight loss doctor. Inside the shower stall was a typical assortment of shampoo, conditioner, body wash, razors, and a loofah.

Entering the bedroom, I was once again impressed and a little jealous of the setup. In the center of the room was a queen-size bed with matching nightstand on either side - each with matching lamps. At twenty-five, Stephanie was certainly a grown-up. In comparison, I felt like I was still living the life of a college student with my one dresser and a small kitchenette in a room in someone else's big house. Stephanie was living in luxury compared to what I had. Definitely jealous.

Originally, I had started renting rooms and moving every few months to avoid any repercussions from the human traffickers I tried to take down a few years ago. Those traffickers killed my boyfriend Brendon but were never caught, and I held the fear they would come after me too. The traffickers told me to drop the case, or they would kill my boyfriend. I couldn't conceive that it would actually happen, but when it did, my world crumbled. Ever since then, I looked over my shoulder and tried not to get too close to others in case they wanted to take out another one of my loved ones. Martina and Dee had finally convinced me I needed to stop living like that. They thought the traffickers were likely long gone and wouldn't come after me or my family, but I wasn't as convinced. I supposed I was small potatoes compared to other enemies they had. Still, I worried. My therapist had also explained that it was no way to live and that by continuing to hide away from those who loved me, the traffickers were winning. Maybe moving into an actual apartment would be part of my reawakening - my new beginning. My fresh start.

Refocusing on the bedroom, I turned to the closet and began sifting through the clothing on the hangers. Stephanie had items ranging from slacks to party dresses. Checking the tags, I noted the clothing right in front of me was all size six, but a bunch of other garments pushed to the back of the closet had a range of sizes from eight to twelve.

It appeared as if Stephanie proudly displayed the sixes in the center. Had she met her goal weight? Had it been worth it? Assuming, of course, her weight loss efforts had put her in the hospital. We still weren't sure that was the case. But Stephanie had no history of a heart condition or any other life-threatening diseases or illnesses that could have caused her sudden collapse. Although, I knew that if you don't eat enough, you could become dizzy and then fall and hit your head. I didn't see any blood in the bathroom, and Vicki hadn't mentioned a head wound.

I returned to the bedroom. I still had found nothing interesting, but there were always the nightstands. On the right side of the bed, I opened the drawer and found it was a goodie drawer containing some lotions, a vibrator, condoms, and a box of tissues. *Good for her. You don't need a man to be satisfied.* I moseyed over to the other nightstand and pulled open the drawer. *Bingo.* Inside was a stack of journals, along with a pen and a set of flannel pajamas. Hopefully, the diaries would give me some insight into what was going on in Stephanie's life before she collapsed.

Part of me felt bad snooping in Stephanie's belongings. Who knew what I would find? But it was in the spirit of helping Stephanie that I read her diaries. I wasn't trying to invade her privacy, even though as I cracked open the cover of the first journal, that felt like exactly what I was about to do.

Under normal circumstances, I wouldn't read anyone's diary, someone's most inner thoughts. It wasn't fair that I was looking at it, but if it could save her life, it would be worth the invasion. I read to the latest entry and felt like a scummy person for reading it. She was gushing about a guy at work. Sounded like they were getting close. I continued reading this poor woman's internal thoughts, and an earlier entry about feeling dizzy and lightheaded caught my attention. This could be useful.

For the next two hours, I read through all of Stephanie's journals. My heart was heavy for her. The entries only went back a year, but from what I had read, it was a hard year for Stephanie. Things her sister Vicki had not told me about. Maybe she didn't know. If I didn't know any better, I'd say Stephanie was depressed. She seemed to hate her body and herself for not having more control over what she ate or how much she exercised. The amount of pain it caused her - it was no wonder she had sought out the weight loss doctor.

Unfortunately, in the journals, she never mentioned the name of the doctor. But I learned she was at a weight loss center where there were group meetings and counseling and that she was really excited that her weight was changing. Things seemed to have turned around. I shut the last journal and considered what I would do with them.

I set the diaries down and stared at the bathroom again. *Lightbulb moment.* Rushing back to the medicine cabinet, I grabbed the bottle of B12 and unscrewed the cap. I dropped a few of the tablets into my hand. They were stamped B12. I slid the pills back into the bottle and screwed the lid back on and repeated the same with the multivitamin - also stamped. I shook my head and put them back as well.

I unscrewed the vitamin C bottle and put a few tablets in my hand. My pulse quickened. They didn't look like any vitamin C tablets I'd ever seen. They weren't shaped like an orange and didn't have vitamin C stamped on them. They were capsules. Did they sell vitamin C capsules? I opened up the vitamin D container and inspected the pills inside. Small white tablets with no stamping or other type of marking. Not normal. I doubted they were vitamins.

Heart pounding, I realized I got my first break. I grabbed the two containers, vitamin C and vitamin D, and stuffed them into my backpack along with the diaries.

4

SELENA

Vicki was pacing in front of the hospital's main entrance when I walked up from the parking lot. I had called her after I had found the mysterious pills hidden in the vitamin C and vitamin D bottles. She said she didn't know what they were and after Vicki consulted with Stephanie's doctors; they said they could look at the pills and see if they recognized them. With time being of the essence, I drove straight over to the hospital as fast as I could. Approaching Vicki - I could see she had tears in her eyes. Something had happened. Vicki said, "They just took her into surgery. Open heart surgery."

"I'm so sorry." I supposed the type of drugs she'd been taking made little difference at this point, but it still might be important to know. I was no medical professional and couldn't gauge whether the medication would determine if somebody needed heart surgery or not. "Did they say why?"

"It's her heart valves. I guess they're not opening and closing like they're supposed to. I don't know. They say it's heart valve disease or something like that. The doctor says it's strange and that normally it's something they would see in much older patients. They said they were puzzled."

"Are your parents here as well?"

"They're waiting in the surgery unit. The doctors told us they couldn't tell us that she'd make it for sure. It's very serious," Vicki mumbled as tears streaked her cheeks.

This was bad. Very bad. "Did they think the mysterious pills could be related to her heart condition?"

"I told her cardiologist. He said he wasn't sure but that they were definitely interested in knowing what she may have been taking. At the moment, the most pressing issue is to make sure that her... heart doesn't stop." Vicki broke down into sobs.

Was it possible that Stephanie's desire to lose thirty pounds would cost her her life? Why was all this sounding sort of familiar? I wrapped my arms around Vicki to console her. After she stopped crying, she stepped back and asked, "Did you bring the pills?"

"Yes, I have them with me. I also called my stepmother on the way over here, and there's a lab we can have them tested at if the doctors don't recognize them."

"Okay."

"Do you know how long she'll be in surgery?"

"They said it could be a while."

"Can I bring you or your parents anything? Food or coffee maybe?"

Vicki shook her head. "That's nice of you, but I don't think any of us can eat right now."

"All right, well, if that changes, please let me know."

"Thanks. I should get back in there."

I took the cue. As much as she probably wanted to know why her sister ended up in the hospital, she more urgently wanted to be with her family. It was understandable. I pulled out the plastic bag containing a sample of each of the pills I had found in the vitamin bottles and handed them to her. "Give these to the doctor. I found them in the Stephanie's vitamin bottles. I'll get them tested and let you know the results as soon as I can."

"Okay."

"Take care."

She nodded before hurrying back through the automatic doors into the hospital.

I didn't envy Stephanie or her family. If it were my situation and my loved one was in there, I'd be on pins and needles until I knew if they were going to be okay. I turned back and headed toward my car. Glancing at my phone, I checked the time and figured I'd probably still be able to make it over to Stephanie's place of employment to question her coworker about the clinic that she had referred Stephanie to.

I GAVE A FRIENDLY SMILE TO THE RECEPTIONIST AT Danziger Medical Devices. "Hi, my name is Selena, and I'm here to see Karen Hart."

"Is she expecting you?" the perky lady asked.

"No, not exactly."

"What is this pertaining to?"

"I'm actually here representing Stephanie Crawford and her family. I'm not sure if you know Stephanie - but she is in the hospital."

The young woman frowned. "I heard she was in the hospital. Is she doing better?"

I shook my head. "I'm afraid not. Things are still pretty serious." I wasn't sure how much the family wanted me to reveal about Stephanie's condition. Vicki Crawford was my client, and I considered all our dealings confidential unless Vicki explicitly said otherwise.

"Please give my best to the family. And let Stephanie know we're all rooting for her. We miss her. She's a great person."

I said, "That's what I'm hearing."

Stephanie seemed to have everything going for her. And she was well-liked at work - according to the receptionist, anyway. I couldn't wrap my head around why someone who seemed to be so happy on the outside and was loved by family and friends would beat herself up for being larger than a supermodel. It made little sense to me. Although between social media and the movie stars, I supposed it's hard not to compare yourself to those on the screen, both big and small. The more I thought about it, the more I realized I had compared myself to others. It wasn't always on the forefront of my mind, but I checked my reflection in the mirror at least once a day and sometimes in store windows. I didn't like it when I didn't fit into my clothes, and I was proud of my lean, strong body. It was mostly because I worked out a lot and ate healthy, but it still didn't mean that I would be okay with not looking the way I do now.

"Is it possible for me to speak with Karen Hart?" I asked again.

"It's about Stephanie? What do you need to talk to her about? I didn't think they were that close."

"Her sister told me they belonged to the same group and that maybe she could help with information relating to what is wrong with Stephanie. It's important that I speak with Karen. I'd really appreciate it if you could let her know I'm here."

The receptionist nodded. "Of course. Anything for Stephanie."

"Thank you." I stepped back as she presumably called Karen to ask her to come out. The receptionist spoke in a hushed tone, and I couldn't make out anything she said.

Hopefully, Karen could give me the information I needed. And, hey, maybe she even knew what the pills were. The receptionist hung up the phone. "Karen will be right out. So, you know the family?"

"I know her sister, Vicki. She's asked me to look into some activities Stephanie was into before she collapsed."

"Have you found anything interesting?"

"Not yet," I lied.

"I hope you do. It makes me sick to think that Stephanie is lying in a hospital unconscious."

Imagine if she knew that Stephanie at twenty-five was being rushed into open heart surgery. It was bizarre, and I could understand why her family had been so concerned. The door to the left opened, and a very thin woman with honey colored hair pulled back into a ponytail appeared. "Are you Selena?"

"Yes, I'm Selena. Are you Karen Hart?"

"Yes. You're here to ask questions about Stephanie?"

"That's right."

Karen looked both left and right before she said, "We should speak outside."

I waved to the receptionist, mouthed 'thank you', followed Karen back to the entrance of the company, and exited.

Out in the cold air, I could see my breath as I exhaled. Karen wrapped her arms around her shoulders. She hadn't brought a jacket outside with her. "What questions do you have for me about Stephanie?"

"I'm here on behalf of Stephanie's family. Her sister Vicki asked me to talk to you about a weight loss center you had recommended to Stephanie. Can you tell me more about that?"

"It's not a weight loss center. It's an eating disorder clinic. What does that have to do with her being in the hospital?"

Eating disorder clinic? "It may not be related, but we're trying to figure out what could've caused her sudden collapse. We also want to understand any activities she was taking part in. I couldn't find any records for the clinic at her apartment, but her sister said you were the one who referred her."

Karen glanced around the building and across at the parking lot. "I referred her."

"What is the name of the center?" I asked.

"Teeling's Clinic."

"Do you go to Teeling's Clinic?"

"I used to. I don't anymore."

"Why not?"

"Well, I met my goal weight. So, I didn't need to go back."

That didn't make any sense. Why would an eating disorder clinic release you after you hit your goal weight? Shouldn't there be ongoing counseling? "Had Stephanie met her goal weight?"

"I think so. She was looking absolutely fantastic. She was turning heads around the office."

My thoughts drifted back to Stephanie's journals. What an invasion of her privacy for me to read every thought she'd had. But there was one in particular about a man at work who she was interested in. That likely had nothing to do with her collapse, but it must be what Karen was referring to. "Anyone in particular?"

"Chuck and her were getting pretty cozy. Rumor has it they have a thing going."

"Really?"

"Well, they've definitely been spending their lunch time together. I'm not sure if it's progressed outside of the office."

There was no mention of dating in Stephanie's diaries. "So, is there anything else you can tell me about this clinic... you said it's an eating disorder clinic?"

"That's right. It's a really great place. Dr. Teeling is super nice and really caring. He has group sessions, and we go through counseling to help us get over some of our eating issues. I just simply wanted to lose weight, but there're women who go there for many reasons. Some have eating disorders and they're trying to get healthy. I don't see how it would have anything to do with Stephanie's collapse. It's a place of healing."

An interesting take on the clinic. Based on Stephanie's journals, she was unhappy with her size before her sudden weight loss - it was eating her alive, so to speak. But other than that, Vicki had mentioned no history of anorexia, bulimia, or any other eating disorder.

"Does the doctor prescribe any drugs to help with weight loss?" I asked.

Karen paled. "No. He recommends we take vitamins to keep us healthy, but that's it."

"Anything else you can tell me about the clinic?"

"That's about it. How is Stephanie doing?"

"It's still pretty serious."

"That's awful. Please let her family know I'm thinking of her. Everyone here is. She's one of those women in the office everybody likes, you know?"

"I do. I'll deliver the message. Thank you for your time."

I watched as she shivered and headed back into the warmth of the office.

Karen Hart had insisted the clinic was a place of healing. She herself had been a patient at the clinic and had lost weight, met her goal, and seemed perfectly fine. Maybe Stephanie had a heart condition the family just never knew about. After speaking to Vicki the day before, I had searched the internet for heart conditions, and what I read was that you could have one for your whole life, and until something went wrong, you wouldn't know about it. Was there really something nefarious at the Teeling's Clinic? What were those pills inside the vitamin bottles? Had they come from the clinic?

5

STEPHANIE, AGE 12

BLUE SEQUINS GLITTERED UNDER THE DEPARTMENT STORE lights. I grabbed the hanger and rushed over to the mirror and held the dress up against my body. I loved it. It was sparkly, like a fairy. I was going to my very first school dance and was so excited because not only was it seventh graders but it was eighth graders too. I couldn't wait to get dressed up with my best friends. Giggling from behind me caught my attention. "Janine, Tammy, what is it?"

Janine lifted a dark green ball gown and twirled around. "What do you think about this for the dance?" She laughed.

"I think it's perfect for you."

Janine said, "Me too."

It was ridiculous for a seventh, eighth-grade dance. It wasn't a formal dance. Janine hung the ball gown back on the rack and said, "Oh, my gosh, that's so pretty. Have you tried it on yet?"

"Not yet. I want to. Did you two find anything?"

Janine said, "Not yet, but there's so many cool dresses. I think I want a sparkly dress, too."

Tammy said, "Me three!"

I said, "Oh, my gosh. I have an idea. Let's grab a bunch of dresses and put on a fashion show."

Janine proclaimed, "Yes!"

Tammy said, "Heck yeah!"

The three of us scoured the racks for the best of the best and hurried over to the dressing room where my mom sat reading a magazine. She was cool enough to offer to take the three of us dress shopping. Janine and Tammy's moms gave them a budget and had worked it out with Mom to buy the ones they wanted and then their moms would reimburse her.

We hid behind each of the curtains in our individual dressing rooms. After slipping into the blue sparkly dress, I stared into the mirror, and my lips parted. I loved it. I looked like a princess - a semi-formal princess. This was definitely the dress I wanted. I reached behind me and tugged at the zipper. It wouldn't budge. I'd need a bigger size.

"Are you ready yet?" Janine asked.

I said, "Not yet. I need a bigger size."

Mom said, "Hand me the dress. I'll get you another size."

After slipping off the perfect dress, I pushed aside the drape and handed Mom the dress. She looked at the size on the label - hesitated - and said, "I'll be right back."

I put the next dress on and hated it. I looked like a baby doll. Stepping out of my dressing room, I watched as Janine and Tammy twirled around in their extravagant ball gowns.

This continued for several more dress changes before Mom returned with the other size. She handed it to me and whispered, "It's a nine, but don't worry, we can cut out the tag." She gave me a reassuring smile before returning to her chair.

Why did we need to cut out the tag? Was size nine big? Too big? Now that I thought about it, Janine and Tammy had both grabbed size threes. Stripped down to my underwear, I glanced down at my legs and my stomach and my arms. I supposed I was bigger than Janine and Tammy. Was that bad? Did I need to go on a diet? Did I need to count calories like Mom?

I slipped on the dress and reached around to the zipper and got it up halfway. I then reached over my head and arched my back to zip it all the way up. Straightened out, I stared in the mirror. I loved the dress.

My mom called out from the other side of the dressing room. "Stephanie, are you ready to show us?"

Janine said, "Prepare to be dazzled."

I pushed aside the curtain and walked out.

Mom nodded with a wide grin. "You look gorgeous, Stephanie."

"Can I get it?" I asked.

"Let's see how much it costs." I walked closer to Mom, and she looked at the tag. "I think that's doable. Let's get it."

"Seriously?" I asked, in awe.

"Of course. It's your first dance. You have to have the best dress imaginable."

Mom was the best. I didn't want to say that in front of my friends, but she really was. We changed back into our regular clothes and met Mom at the register with our selections. With excitement, I handed the dress to her to give to the clerk. I couldn't wait for the dance to arrive so I could wear it.

6

SELENA

BACK IN MY OFFICE, I PULLED UP THE WEBSITE FOR THE lab that Martina had told me about. We needed to find out what those pills were that Stephanie had concealed in the vitamin bottles. Martina had given me the name of a lab to test them, but she hadn't explicitly stated what tests I'd be asking for. As I read their scope of analysis, I realized I may need a little help. The website said they tested many types of substances like pills, powders, plant materials, and liquids and then listed the tests that could be ordered. The only problem was I didn't know what GC MS was or microscopic analysis or FT IR or LC MS or HPLC. I had no idea which one I needed and realized I should have taken more chemistry and science classes during my time in college, but they didn't align with my major in criminal justice with a minor in business. *Ah-ha.* That gave me an idea. I knew a delightful and brilliant chemistry major who was also my best friend. I picked up the phone and called Dee. After one ring, she picked up. "Hey, Selena, what's up?"

"Hi, Dee. I thought I could use your scientific expertise for something I'm working on."

"I'm intrigued. What is it?"

"Well, I can't give you all the details of the thing I'm working on, but I have some pills, and I need to know what's in them. The lab website I'm on says they do different types of substance testing, but I really don't know which one to request. To me, it just looks like a bunch of letters."

"What kind of pill is it? A capsule or a tablet?"

"One is a tablet, and one's a capsule."

"You'll probably want GC MS and maybe a follow-up with HPLC for quantitation."

"Okay, I don't even know what any of that means, but if you say so..."

Dee laughed. "GC MS is gas chromatography mass spectrometry. What the lab does is inject the sample into a machine, and the machine tells them the size of the compound, and then they compare it to a library of other compounds to see which one it matches up with. They'll confirm with a second type of chromatography method like HPLC, or high-performance liquid chromatography, and also determine how much of the drugs are in the pills."

Dee was definitely one of my smartest friends. She was a chemistry major who was planning to go on to medical school to be a psychiatrist for victims of violent crimes. Not only was she my best friend, but she had been my roommate too - until I went out on my own. She herself was a survivor. Our freshman year, she had been attacked, but instead of letting it destroy her, she turned her experience into something positive and started working at the counseling center on campus and changed her career goals to be a therapist for those who had gone through similar experiences. And even more miraculously, she had a boyfriend. Not something I managed to hold on to after my disastrous and heartbreaking boyfriend experiences. But I was happy for her. She was one of the greatest people I knew. "Okay, thanks, Dee. How are things going? How's school?"

Dee still had to finish up the semester before she graduated. We were the same year, but I graduated a semester early during what I was calling my isolation period - away from friends and family - I doubled my course load to get out early so that I could start my career.

"Great. I just got home from school, and now I'm about to change and get ready to go out with Steve."

Steve was Dee's police officer boyfriend whom she met while teaching self-defense courses. They seemed to be pretty happy together. I was happy for her. Her love life was certainly more active than mine - not that I was looking for one.

"Sounds fun."

"How's Vicki's sister's case?" Dee asked.

Dee had referred Vicki to me. I'd thanked her graciously the day before. I was happy to work on something other than just a background check. "It's going."

"How's Stephanie doing?"

"It's pretty serious. She's currently undergoing open-heart surgery."

"How awful."

"Yes. It is. But I'll let you go. Since you've got a date with Steve," I said, emphasizing his name to tease her.

"You know Steve has a friend..." Dee hinted.

"Let me get through this case, and maybe I'll consider it."

Dee cheered. "Yeah."

When Dee and I had met our freshman year, after she'd been assaulted, neither of us thought we'd ever date again. Time was a funny thing.

I said, "All right, I'll talk to you later." I refocused my attention on the screen.

Clicking through the site, based on my advice from Dee, sure enough, she was right. The catalogue described *drug quantitation of pharmaceutical ID by GC MS in quantitation by*

HPLC. It sure was useful to have smarty-pants friends. I continued reading and stopped. *Dang it.* It said the analysis could take up to two weeks. Two weeks was a long time, especially since Stephanie was barely clinging to life in the operating room. I needed a rush job. Who knew if her doctors could identify the pills based on the tablets I gave to Vicki at the hospital. I wanted to call to find out if they had, but I needed to give Vicki and her family some space, as I was sure they were waiting anxiously for the doctor to tell them how Stephanie did during the surgery.

A knock on the door made me nearly jump out of my seat. I glanced up and through the glass door; it was a friendly face. Martina waved as she pushed open the door. "I hope I didn't startle you."

"Just a little. I was studying the website for the analytical test services to get those pills tested."

"Any luck?"

"To be honest, I had to call Dee to get some of this deciphered."

Martina nodded. "Smart. Anything I can help with?"

"Well, it's saying here it could take up to two weeks to get the analysis complete. You wouldn't know how to get it done faster?"

"If you call them, they could do a rush job for you. It'll cost more, though."

More costs. In my business class, I had put together a business plan, and I had enough savings to give me one year to turn a profit on my business before I had to get a part-time job, something I really didn't want to do. The retainer from Vicki and her family was sizable, but I didn't want to blow through all of it on testing. I had to account for my time, surveillance equipment, and any fees associated with my undercover work at the clinic. Not to mention any other expenses that could pop up as I tried to find out what happened to Stephanie. I grimaced. "Any idea how much it will cost?"

"It's a few hundred dollars."

Ouch. "I'll call them when they reopen tomorrow."

"Everything okay - financially?"

"It'll be fine. Don't worry about it. And not that I'm not happy to see you, but - why are you here?"

"I was on my way home, and I drove by and saw your light was still on. So, I thought I'd stop in and see how you're doing and how the investigation is going."

Martina was my stepmother, my mentor, and kind of my rock, too. But was she checking up on me? Did she think I needed her help? I was a grownup. I mean, not that I wasn't grateful for everything she had done for me. The fact that I was sitting in this office at all was thanks to her and my dad, who rented the place for an entire year as my graduation gift. "I have it covered." I pushed extra confidence into my tone.

"Anything you want to run by me, just as a sounding board? You know, it's something we do at the firm all the time. We like to bring other investigators in to get ideas about how we should run a case. Not that I don't think you can do it on your own. You're more than capable, but I know working by yourself can be a little lonely."

She was right, and I'd only been working by myself for two days now. "Well, I'm getting the pills tested, and I'm gonna make an appointment at the clinic to get in there and see what it's really like."

She sat down and gave me a quizzical look. "What's your cover story gonna be? You don't look like you need to lose weight."

"Well, I spoke with one of Stephanie's coworkers today, and apparently, the center isn't for weight loss, it's an eating disorder clinic. There're women there who suffer from anorexia, bulimia, and other eating disorders who attend counseling at the center - so I could say I have an eating disorder."

"Which eating disorder are you planning to say you have?"

Good question. I needed to think about this more. "I haven't done a ton of research, but I know a little about anorexia and bulimia..."

Martina said, "Maybe do some more research. If he's an actual doctor and knows what he's doing, he'll spot the lie immediately. You have no signs of an eating disorder. You have a pleasant glow to your skin and muscle tone. Not hallmarks of an eating disorder."

"Can I say I'm recovered from my eating disorder, but I'm afraid I'm going to relapse?"

"That could work." But Martina sounded skeptical.

She had a point. "Well, since they offer group counseling. Maybe I can say I'm just looking for a new counselor to make sure I stay healthy like I am now."

"That's a good idea."

"How did the background check case go?" she asked.

"Easy peasy. I'm already done. I sent the client the report last night."

"So, you got your first paycheck." She glowed with pride.

I smiled. "I did." It wasn't very much, but it was a paycheck. Based on my calculations, I only needed, like, fifty more of those.

"I'm headed home. Do you want to come over for dinner?"

"I still have some work to do, but I'll see you on Sunday, okay?"

"Okay. Don't work too hard."

"I'll try."

Martina got up to leave, and I said, "Thanks for coming by, Martina. It's good to see you, and you're right. It's nice to have somebody to talk about cases with."

"Any time."

I waved as she exited.

I favorited the site for the testing lab before searching the web for Teeling's Clinic. As Karen Hart had mentioned, the place offered many services. The rest of the evening would be spent researching a believable eating disorder for myself before making my appointment. I didn't want to blow my cover on day one.

Intrigued by the site, I clicked on the doctor's photo and then conducted a quick Google search for a D. Teeling, MD. The only thing that came up was the Teeling's Clinic website and a website for Teeling Irish Whiskey.

I suspected I'd need a full background on Dr. Teeling. I logged into my background check website account and entered his name. Tapping on the desk with my fingertips, I waited. The results screen popped up. *Hmm. This just got more interesting.* There were no records or medical licenses registered in the state of California for a D. Teeling. I switched back to the website and stared at the photograph next to Dr. Teeling's name. I stared into his dark eyes and asked, "Who are you really, Dr. Teeling?"

7

SELENA

Relief filled my being as Vicki explained Stephanie had made it through the open heart surgery and the doctors were hopeful that she would make a recovery, albeit a slow one. "That's great to hear."

"Yes, we're happy that she's going to be all right, but the doctor thinks she'll need physical therapy, medication, and without knowing what caused it, we're not sure if the problem will come back or new symptoms will occur."

"Were the doctors able to identify the pills that I gave you?"

"That's the interesting part. A few of her doctors looked at them, and none of them recognized the pills, but what they agreed on was that they were consistent with street drugs. The doctors don't think they are from any pharmaceutical company, but they thought they looked like somebody was manufacturing them and passing them off as a regulated product."

I was relieved that I could get a rush to the laboratory for testing the pills. Like Martina had said, it cost me a few hundred dollars, but considering the doctors couldn't identify the drugs, it would be worth it.

"The lab said they should be able to do the analysis on the pills within forty-eight hours."

"That's great. Have you been to the weight loss center yet?"

"Not yet, but I plan to look at it today."

"What aren't you telling me?" Vicki asked.

I hesitated on whether to tell her my suspicions since I had nothing firm, but since she was my customer, and they say the customer is always right, I basically gave her everything I had. "I met with Karen Hart yesterday, and she confirmed she referred Stephanie to the Teeling's Clinic. I looked at the website that says it is an eating disorder clinic led by a doctor named D. Teeling. But the thing is, I did some looking into this doctor, and I can't find any records for D. Teeling in California - no licenses. No records at all."

Vicki gasped. "You're kidding? So, this guy is a fraud? I was right. He couldn't be trusted. He may not even be a doctor."

"That's what I'm going to find out. I plan to stake out the clinic and see what I can gather from those coming in and out and hopefully get a glimpse of the doctor or whoever he is. And then I'll try to find his true identity."

"Whoever this guy is, I know in my gut, Selena, that he's who caused my sister to collapse and why my sister had to have open heart surgery. I want to take him down. Can we do that? Can you take him down?" Vicki asked.

"Absolutely." And I meant it. I had picked up some books in the library on eating disorders and diet culture. So far, I didn't like what I read. I still had some research to do, but all signs were pointing to Dr. Teeling being a crook and preying on women and their insecurities about their bodies.

"Thank you, Selena. Please let me know anything you find out."

"Will do. Let me know when Stephanie wakes up. I'd love to talk to her. It could help the investigation."

"I will as soon as she's awake and strong enough."

"Great. You take care." I hung up the phone and shoved it into my backpack. It was going to be a long day, but I had my reading material, and I had a mission.

WITH A BLACK BASEBALL CAP AND SUNGLASSES ON, I SAT back in my car, watching the entrance to the clinic. There wasn't a lot of heavy foot traffic, but from what I'd seen so far, only young women entered and exited the building. They were all sizes and races. Likely, I wouldn't catch sight of the doctor until he was on his lunch break or left for the day, but as soon as he stepped out the doors, I was going to be on him. I would find out who he was and what he was up to. If he was the person giving out the illegal drugs to Stephanie that caused her current condition, I'd expose him, and he would pay for what he did.

I was tired of men thinking they could do whatever they wanted, take whatever they wanted, no matter how it affected women. Over the last four years, I'd learned about some terrible atrocities in the world. Women had been treated as unequal to men since the beginning of time. Between the ridiculously lax domestic violence laws, to victim blaming of sexual assault survivors, to just plain not believing women when they complained about violence or possible violence against them - I was tired of watching marginalized groups treated like second-class citizens, like they were less than human. *Fucking patriarchy.*

I pulled the eating disorder book I had checked out from the library out of my backpack and opened it up to descriptions of the different eating disorders. I still needed to flush out my back story to make sure it was believable enough to infiltrate the clinic. The three most common eating disorders, and often most deadly, were anorexia nervosa, bulimia nervosa, and a lesser known, and lesser talked about, binge eating disorder. After reading the high-level descriptions, I knew Martina was right. I wasn't sure I could pull off anorexia or bulimia unless I said I had been in recovery for quite a while.

Thinking back to Stephanie's journals, it occurred to me that she must have had more diaries than what I had found. Maybe I should return to her apartment and search through the stacks of boxes in her closet. Maybe she had some from her childhood, or from previous years, that would help me better understand what she'd been going through. From what I had read so far, she didn't seem to have anorexia, which the book described as being a complex disorder, so I obviously couldn't be sure. There were so many variations and types of anorexia - like restricting type and binge eating purging types. Fascinated, I continued reading.

After a while, I set the book down and contemplated what I had read about how eating disorders originated. It wasn't what I had thought. From what I read, eating disorders almost always started out as diets, but when the diet turned into a disorder, it was no longer just about food and weight anymore. We lived in a society where at each corner there was a new diet craze. Was that also contributing to the rising number of eating disorders?

Returning my focus to the book, the next disorder I read about might be what Stephanie was struggling with. Binge eating disorder sounded like bulimia but there was no purging. She didn't seem to do any purging, but she definitely counted every single calorie, and when she'd gained a few pounds, she hated herself and her body. But then again, just because she didn't record that she'd been vomiting or taking laxatives didn't mean she wasn't.

The criteria for binge eating disorder included lack of control over eating during an episode. So, like, the whole 'you can't eat just one chip' thing? And second, one must have one of the following: eating more rapidly than normal, eating until feeling uncomfortably full, eating a large amount of food when not feeling physically hungry, or eating alone because of being embarrassed by how much one is eating. Last, feeling disgusted or depressed because of overeating and binge eating events occurring at least two days a week for six months. That sounded a lot like Stephanie's diaries. There was marked distress regarding binge eating in Stephanie's writing. She had verbally beaten herself up each time she ate too much.

It was heartbreaking that someone like Stephanie could hate herself so much - because on all accounts, she seemed like she had a great life, good friends, family, and a good job. She cared so much about what she looked like that it was destroying her self-esteem and maybe even her life.

I didn't understand what caused this - I mean, I understood wanting to look pretty and have positive attention; I guess. Although my history with men was so terrible that I often tried to look more invisible and not stand out. But having female friends, I knew I wasn't the norm. Most women took a lot of time and energy to look their very best, or what society made them believe was beautiful, like being tall, thin, and flawless. Like being flawless was even possible. Perfection was a myth. Something we could never achieve. And why would we? If you asked me, I thought what made people different was what made them interesting. I used to hate being small. At barely five foot three, I had been called munchkin and shorty, and it had bothered me. But it was also what made me different, right? Although I still wouldn't mind being taller, my height gave me an element of surprise with a physical opponent. Looking at my slight frame, you wouldn't expect somebody who could physically fight a man twice my size. *Well, if they don't have a gun or a long sword.*

I guess there's always something about each of us we wished could be different, but my therapist had told me over and over, and I guess I believed it was true, that our differences made us great. What if everybody looked the same and talked the same and was the same? It would be one big, boring world.

I continued reading, trying to figure out why body image and disorders were such a problem. Some experts even went to the extreme of calling eating disorders an epidemic - not only killing women but men too. From what I understood, scientists were still trying to figure out what caused eating disorders and determine if there was a relationship between biological factors and environment. But the biggest risk factor that all the experts seemed to agree on was that eating disorders were fueled by a culture that continued to promote dieting and body image dissatisfaction.

Maybe if it wasn't so profitable for the diet industry, it wouldn't be pushed into our faces so much? Maybe if they promoted campaigns for people to love their bodies, not necessarily for the way they looked but what they did for us, then we'd have a happier society and fewer eating issues?

I glanced over the edge of the book and watched as more women left the clinic. There was no sign of the good doctor. Focus returned to the book, I shook my head as I continued to read about the troubling statistics around eating disorders in our diet culture.

Little girls worrying about their weight, primping in front of the mirror to look like princesses. It suddenly made me think of childhood Disney movies where the princess was being saved by the prince. *Ha. Those were definitely fairytales.* Why do we even put this idea into little girls' heads? Why can't we be our own saviors? *Guess what? No woman needs a man.* If a woman wants a man, that's great, but we certainly don't need them. I don't need them to open doors for me, and I don't need them to buy me things or dinner. I can do that all on my own, and so many other women can, too. Why does society continue to teach young women that we aren't good enough on our own?

My blood pressure was rising at the range of systemic issues of inequality regarding women. I didn't know if it was because I identified as a powerful female or that I knew so many strong women in my life. There was Martina, Dee, and so many others I had come across. Why were we always portrayed as the damsel in distress? Why were women still making less money than men for the same jobs? When would it end? When would men stop trying to tell women how they're supposed to look or how they're supposed to be or how much money they should make or what they should do with their own bodies? When?

After a few cleansing breaths to calm myself down, I figured I could sit here and get angry, or I could do something about it. I wasn't sure how big of an impact I could make on the entire world, but I knew I could take on the supposed Dr. Teeling and find out if he was part of the problem. I was betting he was.

After a few more hours, my stomach rumbled. It was time for another protein bar. From my backpack, I grabbed a bar and unwrapped it while staring out the car window. Chewing the portable sustenance and its chocolate peanut-butter combination, I knew it wasn't the healthiest choice, but when you're on a stakeout, there aren't too many better options. I stopped chewing and set the protein bar down on the passenger seat and picked up my binoculars.

Peering through the lenses, I watched him strolling out into the parking lot. *Bingo.* He was in my sights. I set the binoculars back down and started the car. As he climbed into a silver BMW, I recorded his license plate number as well as the make and model of the car into my phone. After he backed out and drove out of the parking lot, I began my pursuit.

8

STEPHANIE, AGE 15

WALKING TOWARD MY HOUSE, I SPOTTED VICKI'S CAR IN the driveway. With the day I had, I had completely forgotten she was coming home this weekend. I was so glad she was home. Since she went away to college, I missed her almost daily. Lately, it had been a little better when I started dating Tyler, but now - he was gone. I needed my big sister.

I couldn't believe Tyler was seeing Rachel behind my back. He acted like it wasn't a big deal - the words that he'd spewed onto me felt like acid on my skin. He'd said, "It's just run its course. Steph, I'm sure you understand. We had some good times, but I'm with Rachel now." Run its course? What did that even mean? I didn't know how to respond, so I ran away, so he wouldn't see the tears that had formed in my eyes. The tears that seemed to lack an off switch.

After a deep breath, I wiped my eyes and walked up to the front door of our house. I guess I should've known that things with Tyler and me wouldn't last forever. We were only fifteen, and he was my first boyfriend. What were the odds of that lasting forever? Even though I knew that, it hurt so bad it felt like the aching in my chest would never go away. My thoughts of Tyler would never go away. Vicki would know just the right thing to say, I was sure of it.

I tiptoed into the house, shutting the door quietly behind me so I could sneak into the bathroom and clean up my face before I saw Vicki and the rest of the family. I was hoping it was only Vicki at home because I didn't think I could face my mom and dad pretending to be happy or smiling. Dropping my backpack in my room, I snuck into the bathroom to wash my face and splash it with cold water.

Over the faucet, I heard, "Steph, is that you? Are you home?"

I hadn't been as sneaky as I'd thought. "I'm in the bathroom. I'll be right out." After drying off my face, I stared in the mirror. Was I too ugly? Too fat? Was that why Tyler didn't want to be with me anymore? He said he loved me. I believed him. Maybe I was stupid to think someone like Tyler would ever want to be with me. Of course, he was with Rachel. She was tall, blonde, and skinny. A cheerleader. I bet nobody ever offered to cut her tags out of her dresses. My heart hurt, but I knew I couldn't hide from Vicki forever. I made my way out to the kitchen, where Vicki was rummaging through the refrigerator. "Hey, Vicki."

"Hey." Her smile melted. "What's wrong?"

Bowing my head, I was too defeated to pretend like everything was okay. Plus, it didn't seem like anybody else was home. "Tyler and I broke up. He dumped me."

"I'm so sorry, Steph."

I couldn't stop the tears from falling. Why did it hurt so badly? Vicki wrapped her arms around me and told me it would be okay and Tyler was a jerk. That I was too good for him. Shaking my head, I said, "I don't think that's true. If it were, he wouldn't have dumped me for Rachel."

"You're so much better than Rachel. Is she a straight-A

student? Is she super awesome? You are the smartest, most fun, and awesome person I know."

"Then why doesn't he want me?" I asked.

Vicki said, "Because he's stupid - that's why. You know what? I have the cure for this stupid guy. You and I will have a sister night."

"A sister night?"

"Yep. We're going all out. Mom and Dad left us money for dinner. Tonight, we'll go out for pizza and get ice cream and candy. We'll rent movies - we'll rent the best movie *ever*."

"Seriously?" I wasn't sure I felt like leaving the house and facing the rest of the world. A world where Tyler didn't want me anymore.

"Trust me, it will be great. Or we could stay in and get delivery. We'll watch the movie in the bonus room. I'll tell Mom and Dad that we just want a sister night, and they'll leave us alone."

"I'd like that. Thanks."

"You got it. I'll go to the store and stock up on supplies. We'll have the best night ever, and I'm sure you'll forget stupid what's-his-name."

I was so glad Vicki was home. I missed having somebody in my corner. Mom and Dad were, but there was something about having your big sister always there fighting for you. Vicki was the best sister ever.

Later that night, we cozied up on the couch with blankets on our laps while we watched the world's greatest movie, *Clueless*. A pint gripped in my hand, I shoved a mouthful of chubby hubby ice cream into my mouth. The sugar and cream soared through my body in euphoric waves. The more I ate, the better I felt. I even laughed at some of the funnier parts of the movie. After I polished off the tub of ice cream, Vicki said, "Looks like you're ready for candy."

She smiled as she ripped open the box of red vines.

"Thanks, Vicki. You're the best."

"I know," she chirped back.

The more I ate, the better I felt. The red licorice was the perfect blend of sweet and chewy.

The doorbell rang, and Vicki hopped off the couch. "It sounds like the pizza is here. I'll get it - pause the movie, okay?"

"Okay." I pressed pause on the remote.

It was turning out to be one of the best nights instead of one of the worst days with old what's-his-name, which was what Vicki had insisted on referring to him as. I munched on the red vines as Vicki went to get the pizza. When she walked back into the bonus room, the scent of freshly baked dough and pepperoni filled my senses. With the ice cream, the candy, and now pizza, I felt like I had finally found something that took away the pain.

9

SELENA

ADRENALINE PUMPING, I FOLLOWED DR. TEELING'S CAR onto the highway. Thankfully, there were a lot of cars out, so I could follow fairly close behind without being spotted. Assuming he wasn't on the lookout for a tail. But if he wasn't crooked, why would he be looking out for a tail? An innocent man typically wasn't too aware of his surroundings or suspicious that somebody would follow him on a daily basis. Was the good doctor feeling guilty about something? What was he hiding, and who was he hiding it from?

As I followed him down the highway, I ran scenarios through my head. I had to make sure that once I got inside the clinic, I could interact with people who may have crossed paths with Stephanie. It was decided. I would claim to have binge eating disorder - it seemed like the easiest one to fake since people of all sizes had the disorder. It could be believable that I'd been on a diet, so I hadn't binged for a while, which was why I was so fit. It could work, right?

It being the middle of the day, I hadn't expected that the good doctor would take a long lunch, yet we'd been on the freeway for forty minutes. Where was he going? Long lunch or home for the day? It was a bit peculiar. I watched as his silver BMW pulled over to the far right, changing lanes, and then he exited the freeway. I sped up, trying to catch up with his sudden movement off the freeway. Was he on to me, or was he just a careless driver?

We had arrived in the far East Bay. It would be surprising if he were going home. He had his own clinic - why would he give himself such a terrible commute? Off the freeway, there were far fewer cars on the road. It would be more difficult not to be detected. But I could do it. I was going to have to do it.

Soon, the traffic thinned out even more, and I worried there were only two cars on the road. I was going to have to get strategic. It would help if I wasn't lost. I wasn't familiar with the area since I wasn't like the city folk who got excited about driving out on the weekends to go to the local farms to pick my own berries or apples or walnuts. No thanks.

We continued onto a two-lane road. *Great.* There weren't many exits or places for me to get out of there in a hurry if things turned sour. He made a right, and I slowed my car and made the turn when enough time had passed. So far, he didn't appear to be slowing down, or given the impression that he was on to me. *Damn.* Except his sudden right into the only gas station around.

From the move, either Dr. Teeling actually needed gas, or he was trying to lose me. Either way, I didn't want him to see my face. I continued down the road past the gas station as if his stop hadn't thrown apart my entire plan. Had I been seen? Even if he had seen me, between the hat and glasses, I didn't think he would recognize me when I was sitting across from him in an office.

Reality hit me fast. I did not know where I was, and I couldn't exactly pull over to check my phone for directions. Without many options, I continued making right turns until I got back onto the main road. Soon, I was far enough away from Dr. Teeling that I could pull over and look up directions on my phone. Not liking the isolated vibes, I wanted out of there - fast. After consulting my phone, I made my way back to civilization and away from the area that was known for either McMansions or drug dealers and gangs. What on Earth was Dr. Teeling doing out there? Did he live there in his own cookie-cutter house, or was he visiting friends?

BACK INSIDE THE SAFETY OF MY OFFICE, I ENTERED THE doctor's license plate number into the database to access his records. Soon enough, the search results returned. His fancy car was registered to a Douglas Potter with a home address listed in Concord, California. *Hmm. Not the far East Bay where he led me to earlier in the day.* I searched for Douglas Potter's DMV photo. Was D. Teeling Douglas Potter or someone entirely different? The photo popped on my screen, and there was no mistake. Douglas Potter and D. Teeling were the same. If that was the case, Teeling or Potter or whoever he was hadn't been heading home on his lunch break. Where had he been going? And how was Douglas Potter passing himself as off as Dr. Teeling? Who was Douglas Potter?

10

SELENA

AFTER SPENDING THE PREVIOUS EVENING LEARNING everything I could find online about Douglas Potter, I was more determined than ever to take this man down. I now understood that Dr. Teeling was, in fact, Douglas Potter, originally from Naples, Florida, where he grew up and attended Florida State University for undergraduate studies and then got a PhD and MD from the University of Maryland. He had graduated at the top of his class as an endocrinologist and took a position at a top hospital before heading up one of the research departments. From all accounts, Dr. Potter was a brilliant doctor and researcher with a bright future - until he wasn't. Not only was he smart but was greedy too - too greedy for his own good.

According to several news articles I'd found, after five years of leading clinical studies, Dr. Potter had been caught taking bribes from a pharmaceutical company to skew study results - basically falsifying clinical trial information to make the drugs appear safer and more effective than they really were. He was fired, and the state board stripped him of his medical license. If you asked me, I'd say the good doctor had a bit of a moral issue

— as in he didn't have any. Who would pretend a drug was safe, endangering potentially hundreds of thousands of people, just to make a few bucks? As much of the press mentioned, he had been lucky to avoid jail time. After he was barred from practicing medicine, I supposed he was no longer newsworthy because I wasn't able to find any more information about Douglas Potter. And that, I suspected, was because Douglas Potter had become Dr. Teeling and was running an eating disorder clinic in California. And I was about to meet him.

The receptionist called out, "Selena Jones."

I stood up and walked back to the front desk. "I'm Selena Jones."

The very thin woman with heavy makeup said, "Fill out these forms, and Freida will see you soon."

Who was Freida? "I have an appointment with Dr. Teeling."

"Dr. Teeling had a family emergency this morning, so Freida, his assistant, is filling in for him. Don't worry, she's very good."

"Oh, okay. Thanks." Disappointed, I took the clipboard back to my seat and began filling out the forms as I wondered who Freida really was and if she was as shady as Teeling.

After filling out the forms, I pulled out my phone and googled Teeling's Clinic again, hoping to figure out who this Freida person was. When I had looked the night before, I didn't see any mention of her. And what was his family emergency? Was it that Dr. Teeling saw someone following him and now was laying low? Had I rattled the good doctor?

Scrolling through the website, I found no mention of Freida. Maybe she was new?

The door opposite the reception desk opened, and a petite woman with dark hair and dark features called out my name. I stood up and walked toward her. Freida, I presumed. I said, "I'm Selena Jones."

"Nice to meet you. I'm Freida. Why don't you come back to my office, and we can talk."

I followed the woman down the corridor. On my left, there was a shut door with Dr. Teeling etched on the nameplate. Was he in there pretending to not be there? Was it locked? We continued past until we reached an office with an open door. "Please have a seat, Selena."

I sat down, setting my backpack on the ground next to me.

"I read your intake information. It looks like we could get you in here pretty quick. It sounded like it was maybe an emergency for you?"

Nodding, I said, "Yeah, my old therapist moved, and I'm having all these feelings, and I keep wanting to binge, you know?"

"I see. Can you tell me more about your history with your disorder? It says here that you were diagnosed with binge eating disorder?"

"That's right. It was a few years ago. I've been in treatment for a year. My old doctor helped me with different calming techniques. So, instead of eating when I'm stressed or angry or sad or really feeling any emotion at all, instead of grabbing a pint of Häagen-Dazs, I hit the treadmill. Then, of course, that became an issue since I did that too much too. She said that I had traded my binge eating for binge exercising. She explained that I still had binge eating disorder but that I was bordering on potentially developing anorexia. It's so hard. I just want to look good and feel good, you know?" I didn't know if she was believing my story as she peered across the desk. She seemed to be genuinely listening, as if she cared. I knew she could tell that my face was thinner, but I had attempted to bulk up with a few sweaters. Thankfully, it was February, and it was cold enough to wear two sweaters and not totally overheat.

"Can you tell me about your current triggers? What brought you in today?" Freida asked.

I thought back to Stephanie's diaries for a trigger for when she would start eating and then she couldn't stop. "Well, I was up for a promotion at work, but I didn't get it. I was so angry and frustrated, I just wanted to eat an entire bag of chips or a pint of ice cream and a pizza. I knew then I needed to find a new therapist."

Freida continued to have the same supportive look in her eyes. She sat almost perfectly still as she watched my every move. "And how long have you been in recovery? You seem very healthy. You look healthy."

"It's been about six months. My weight has been fluctuating a little up and down, but mostly, things have been going well in my life. I had my doctor until recently. My spiral after not getting the promotion had me scared that I was sliding back. I realized I needed to find a new clinic."

"During your sessions with your doctor - I'm not sure I'm familiar with this doctor you have listed on your form." Freida continued to read my intake forms on the computer screen.

"She's out of state. We used to do virtual calls after she moved out of state, but then she discontinued that service." Was that believable? I sure hoped so.

"During your therapy, did you find the source of your disorder? What caused it or a potential cause?" She crossed her arms and studied me.

Here goes. "It started when I was young. My parents are divorced, and I didn't see my dad for the longest time. My mom was usually busy with her boyfriends, and sometimes they weren't very nice to me or to my mom." *Understatement of the century.* "Sometimes she would leave me alone for long periods of time. I would get scared and lonely. The only thing that made me feel better was to eat. Mom wasn't around much, but she always made sure I had food." A lie. My mom was an alcoholic who could barely care for herself, let alone me.

"Are you still in touch with your mother? Have you been able to heal that family bond? Did she attend sessions with you?"

"No, my mother passed a few years back." *Not a lie.*

"I'm so sorry, Selena."

"Thank you." Martina, my stepmother and amazing private investigator security consultant, told me any good back story was weaved with truths amongst the falsities. It is easy to find trauma in my past to use as leverage for my investigations. Truth was, I had a therapist, but she hadn't moved away, and we didn't do virtual sessions, and it wasn't for an eating disorder.

"If I've got this right, you are healthy right now, but you're feeling like you're on the verge of relapsing. Do you know what kind of support you'd like to receive? Are you open to one-on-one counseling or group therapy? We offer both here at the center. I've found the combination of one-on-one and group therapy can be most effective. It's good to hear from your peers who are going through similar things that you're going through. You're not alone, Selena. We will do everything we can to help you."

I shifted in my seat, suddenly feeling a bit guilty. This woman seemed to be very caring. Or maybe she was just as good an actor as I was? Was I a good enough actor to pretend that I had the same problem as other people who attended the meetings? Would they feel betrayed when they learned the truth? Or if they learned the truth? "Yes, I think that would be helpful. I really don't want to relapse because I just don't want to get fat. Or feel out of control."

"Well, I think you've come to the right place."

"Glad to hear it. So, when's the next group session?"

"We actually have one today. I'll give you a schedule. You're welcome to join today's meeting. In the future, we ask that you sign up ahead of time so that we have enough room and enough counselors. Usually the group is around fifteen to twenty, depending on who shows up. It's a great group of people. I think you'll get along well with them."

"Great."

We continued to speak about my past and my future. I wondered if I needed to speak to my therapist about this whole undercover operation. Obviously, I'd leave out some details, but I was feeling a little guilty and anxious about being in a group setting where other people were baring their souls.

After thanking Freida, I headed back out to the waiting room. The group session for binge eating disorders didn't start for another forty-five minutes, but it didn't make sense for me to leave now. And it didn't seem like I could sneak into Dr. Teeling's office with so many people around.

Taking a seat in the lobby, I hoped to chat up some visitors, but over twenty minutes, nobody entered or exited, so I headed toward the group session room, which Freida had graciously offered to allow me to wait in. It was best anyhow. That way, I might meet some people before the session and try to get the inside scoop. I walked up to the receptionist. "Hi, I plan to attend the BED group session today. Freida said I could wait in the session room. Can you give me directions?"

"Of course. Just head down that hall there. It's the first door on the right. Can't miss it."

"Thanks." I continued down the hall and as the receptionist had said, there was a door open on the right with a sign that read BED Group Session. I stepped inside, and my pulse quickened. There was a man huddled close to a woman - obviously engaged in a secret conversation. They both turned to look at me as my footsteps fell on the linoleum. The greasy man in scrubs asked, "Can I help you?"

"I'm here for the group session. I'm a little early. Freida said I could wait in here. If that's okay? I don't want to interrupt anything."

"No problem. Take a seat, any seat." He whispered something to the woman. The woman nodded, and the man left without another word.

The whole interaction was suspicious. As I sat in a padded chair, the woman came over and took the seat next to me. "You're here for the BED session, too?"

I nodded. "Yep. First time."

"I'm Reba. I've been coming here for about three months."

Perfect. She has to have known Stephanie. "I'm Selena..." But before I could begin questioning Reba more about her time at the clinic and whether she knew Stephanie, another few women strolled in.

Reba said, "Hey, ladies, we've got a new one. This is Selena."

The taller of the two women said, "Hey, Selena. I'm Deirdre."

"I'm Candice. Welcome. I've been coming for ten weeks now and can tell you it's amazing."

"That's great to hear. I'm really looking forward to it. A coworker referred me here. Her name is Stephanie. Did you know Stephanie?"

They exchanged glances. Deirdre said, "Yes, she hasn't been here in almost a week. Is she okay?"

I explained, "No, she's not okay."

The three women exchanged glances once again. Deirdre's brows knitted together, and I could tell she was about to say something when Freida walked in. "Hey, ladies. It looks like you're getting to know our newest member."

Reba said, "Yes."

"Hope you're making her feel at home."

I said, "They are," and glanced over at Deirdre. She gave me a knowing look. Freida chatted us up, but my focus was on Deirdre. I had a feeling she knew something about what happened to Stephanie, but what?

11

SELENA

FIDGETING IN MY SEAT, I LISTENED CAREFULLY AS FREIDA began the group session. "Good morning, warriors."

Mumblings of good morning ran throughout the room. There were about twenty people seated in a circle. Of all the people attending, there were only two males. They were young, still, with a sparkle in their eyes. Maybe in their teens?

Freida said, "Some of you may have noticed we have a new member. Let's give a warm welcome to Selena."

I raised my hand as if waving hello. Twenty mutterings of "Welcome, Selena" swam around me.

After that was done, Freida continued, "Each session, we start off with sharing some wins and then some challenges. Who will start us off with a win?"

A boy with acne and braces said, "I did really good this week. This weekend, I went to the movies but instead of getting the largest bucket of popcorn, I ordered a small, and I didn't even eat all of it. I had enough to enjoy the taste, and then I set it aside. I didn't even think about it again through the rest of the movie. It was nice to walk out of the movie theater knowing I hadn't binged."

"How did that make you feel?" Freida asked.

"It felt good to not feel guilty for eating an entire day's worth of calories in one sitting. I felt like I enjoyed the movie more and didn't hate myself afterward."

A lot of murmurs of agreement filled the space. It was as if they had all been there. Had I been there? No, not really. I had never been that big of an eater, but I had a bit of a sweet tooth, and I liked my coffee.

"Who else would like to share?" Freida asked.

Reba smiled. "Yesterday, I had an enormous challenge. It's where I have the most problems, really."

A woman I didn't know called out, "Grocery store." A few others chuckled.

Reba continued, "Yep, you guessed it. I went grocery shopping yesterday. Every time I go down the junk food aisles, I want everything. I want all the cookies, all the crackers, the chips, the cereal, the ice cream... I could go on. I wanted it all, and I swear the urge doesn't go away. But I stopped myself. Like Freida suggested, I made a list before I entered the store, and I stuck to the list. I only bought what was on my list. When I got home, I felt like I had just won a contest or climbed a mountain." She ended with a smile.

"That's great, Reba. Sounds like you've made real progress."

"I think so. It's nice to leave the grocery store and not feel like a failure."

My heart broke for Reba. I couldn't imagine the grocery store ever becoming traumatizing, but for Reba, it had been.

Suddenly, I was grateful I didn't have an eating disorder or those daily struggles. In the past, I had assumed I was broken inside and that I would always be trying to fix myself. My therapist told me I had made substantial progress over the years, but I wasn't sure if I really believed it. Hearing the wins made me realize how much we never knew what someone else was going through.

These women's and this boy's story of their successes made me realize just how much they were struggling with things that I viewed as small everyday activities but for them were monumental tasks - hurdles to overcome. I never thought of eating disorders as being this difficult, but it was obvious to me they struggled every minute of every day.

"Would anybody else like to share a win this week?"

Candice said, "I joined a gym. And I have walked for thirty minutes on the treadmill every day for the last three days."

The group began snapping their fingers. I guess that's what you did when you congratulated somebody. Snap.

"And how does that make you feel?" Freida asked.

Candice replied, "It felt good to be moving, but to be honest, I felt embarrassed, and I worried people were looking at me thinking 'Look at that fat girl on the treadmill. There's no way she'll ever run on it'."

"Sounds like it might've been a win but also maybe a struggle?" Freida asked.

Candice said, "Yeah, I guess so. But by the time I left the gym, I felt good, so I guess it's more positive than negative."

"I'd say so. Good for you for taking care of yourself and your body. It'll take some time to not think that other people are judging you. I think you're amazing, and I think you're a warrior."

Candice gave a sheepish grin and said, "Thank you."

"Any other wins anyone wants to share today?"

Heads shook throughout the room, as if nobody had any more wins.

"Okay. Who wants to talk about some struggles and the challenges that they've had since the last time we met?"

Deirdre said, "You guys might have noticed I haven't been

here in about a week. I had a hard week." She paused and raised her upper arm and pulled back her sweater sleeves. Her wrists were bandaged. "I found my life to be just a little too over-whelming. This past week, I binged. In a matter of two hours, I'd eaten an entire pizza, a pint of ice cream, a bag of barbeque chips, and a bag of M&Ms. Afterward, I felt so awful and so hopeless that I would never be thin or pretty and that nobody would ever love me." Tears streamed down Deirdre's face. "I thought my life would never get better. I slit my wrists, and if my mom hadn't come in and rushed me to the hospital when she did, I wouldn't have made it. The doctors kept me in the hospital all week. They diagnosed me with major depressive disorder. I just don't know how I'm going to keep going on. I'm not sure I'll ever beat this."

One woman rushed to the back of the room and grabbed a box of Kleenex and brought it over to Deirdre. The woman sat down, still holding the box of Kleenex.

The woman who brought the tissues said, "Deirdre, I've been there too. All I can say is it gets better. It can get better, and know we'd miss you if you were gone."

Deirdre said, "Thanks."

"Deirdre, thank you for sharing that with us. That must've been very difficult. Remember to take it one day at a time. When things are getting too hard, you can always call me or one of you buddies here. Please know you are worthy of love and happiness."

The room remained silent. It was gut-wrenching that these women wanted to die because they didn't look a certain way and felt that they couldn't be loved just because of how they looked. A pit in my stomach grew and grew. I felt awful for these women and wondered if that's how bad it was for Stephanie too - and so many other women and men trying to live up to an ideal that may never be achieved. To think that they had to look a certain way to be loved. I felt like a monster pretending that I felt the same way and had the same problems as them. I had to remind myself it was to help Stephanie because the last thing these people needed was to be betrayed by someone. But I wouldn't betray them. I would help them if I could. If Dr. Teeling was doing something bad, something that caused Stephanie's heart condition, he could do it to the others as well.

I sat through another thirty minutes of heart-breaking stories about people feeling inadequate and guilty and sad that they couldn't control their eating and how they felt like less of a person because of it. This was not what I had anticipated when I walked into that room. I hoped to find out what happened to Stephanie and fast. I didn't want these people to suffer any more than they needed to.

After the session concluded, Reba, Deirdre, and Candice approached me. Deirdre asked, "How did you like the session? You don't have to share right away. It's just important to be there and listen."

I met Deirdre's fierce gaze. "Thanks. I'm sorry about what happened to you."

"It's not my first attempt. This was just the first time that I got far enough that they took me to the doctor. Don't worry about me. I'll be okay."

Candice said, "Hey, do ya'll want to grab coffee? Maybe a bite to eat?"

"Selena, do you want to join us?" Deirdre asked.

"Sure." *Perfect.* I was in and hopefully about to find out more about Stephanie and those pills. Chances were, I needed to be away from the center to get the truth. What would I learn from these women?

12

STEPHANIE, AGE 18

WE LAUGHED AS WE STUCK OUR TONGUES OUT FOR THE photographer. We were supposed to be nice young ladies, but it was our senior prom, and we had let our hair down, and we were having the time of our lives. For the last two weeks, I had done nothing but study for finals and make sure I was at my lowest weight. I'd consumed nothing but meal replacement shakes, water, and coffee. The strict diet had meant no pre-graduation partying or fun dinners out. That night, in my perfectly-fitting gown, I knew my sacrifice had been worth it. A familiar male voice said, "Hey, gorgeous."

The three of us broke away from the photographer, and I stepped toward my sweetie. "Hey, Bill."

He grabbed me around the waist and pulled me closer. I felt so lucky to have the greatest boyfriend ever. We were both seniors and headed off to the same college in the fall. I was on top of the world. I was eighteen, graduating high school soon, and I was with the love of my life. It was like the world was ours. And tonight was the night I was going to give myself to Bill. I had wanted to wait until senior prom to lose my virginity to him. It was time, and I loved Bill, and I knew we'd be together for a long time. We had just celebrated our one-year anniversary, and I had never been more in love. All boys before him were nothing. Not only did I love him, but he had told me he loved me, too.

After a deep kiss, Bill led me out to the dance floor. We danced the night away, and when the music stopped, Bill took my hand and led me up to our hotel room. Mom thought I was staying over at my bestie's, but Bill had reserved a hotel room for us, and I knew everything was going to be perfect. He unlocked the door and stepped inside, gesturing toward the bed. It was king-size and covered in red rose petals. Bill was so romantic. How did I ever get so lucky? With the door closed behind us, he grabbed me, and we kissed, the most passionate kiss I had ever experienced in my life. From there, it was all a blur of blissful perfection.

LYING NEXT TO HIM UNDER A CRISP WHITE SHEET, everything was right in my world. Bill turned on his side and stared deep into my eyes. "Stephanie, you are so wonderful."

"You're wonderful," I gushed.

"I'm so happy to be here with you."

I was the luckiest person on the planet. And I had the most perfect boyfriend. He ran his hand over my belly and quickly removed it. He said, "You know, I've been thinking maybe you and I can start working out together. We can both get fit."

My smile faded. Had he thought I was still too fat? Is that why he was suggesting we work out together and get fit? I had been practically starving myself for two weeks, and I still wasn't good enough. It was obvious I needed to work harder on my body. I couldn't lose Bill.

13

SELENA

Sitting across from my new binge eating disorder friends, uneasiness filled me once again. I hated the fact I was conning them when they all had serious disorders. If the situation was reversed, I would be furious if there was a person who had befriended me pretending to suffer from PTSD just to gain information. I'd be angry. But I supposed if I knew their motivations, like trying to help Stephanie and maybe others, that maybe I would understand *or* I would be fighting mad. I'd like to think I'd be understanding.

Deirdre said to me, "Looks like you've been in recovery for a while."

"I have. But those donuts by the counter sure look good."

Candice said, "I know, right. I have learned in the program that one donut is okay, but two dozen isn't. That's where I struggle - eating only one."

"Same." I would never eat two dozen donuts, but I hoped to find some common ground with them and maybe make them feel better and selfishly redeem myself from tricking these lovely people.

"Where are you from, Selena?" Reba asked.

"I'm from Southern California, but I just moved up here last month."

"Are you missing all the blonde beach babes?" Reba asked.

I cracked a smile. "No. I don't really miss the beach. I was always so self-conscious, wearing a bathing suit," I added for believability.

"Bathing suit." Candice cracked into laughter. "I haven't been in a bathing suit since I was ten. There is no way I'd let people see me in a bikini."

Why do we have to make people feel so bad about their bodies they won't even go swimming or put on a swimsuit?

Reba said, "My last therapist told me I needed to find a way to love myself, regardless of what I look like or what size I am. Wouldn't that be nice?" She scoffed.

Ouch. The pain these women went through was devastating. "I think we can get there, right? I've been reading online about this new movement called body neutrality. Have you heard of it?" I asked.

The three women shook their heads.

"From what I understand, body neutrality is when you focus more on what your body does. Like when you're walking on the treadmill, you are grateful for being strong enough to walk. Or when you're able to lift something heavy or when you can plank for thirty seconds or whatever it is - it is appreciating your body and not so focused on what it looks like - just what it does for you."

Reba said, "I certainly like that idea. I just wish the rest of the world also valued us for what our bodies can do and not what we look like. It would be a lot easier if we didn't get dirty looks or body shamed when we want to eat French fries."

Candice added, "Oh, I know. I'm so sick of the stares whenever I go out to eat. People look at me like I'm some sort of monster for ordering food."

Had I ever done that? Had I ever judged somebody who was larger than average when they'd ordered an unhealthy meal? I hoped not. And if I did before, I certainly would never do it again. The world didn't need me judging them or their appearance. I said, "Yeah, seriously. I mean, we're a lot more valuable than just what we look like."

Reba said, "Exactly. What do you do for a living, Selena?"

Not a private investigator. "I'm in HR."

"Me too. What did you study?" Reba asked.

"Business. I just graduated last month."

Reba nodded. "That's cool."

"What do you ladies do?" I asked.

"I'm a student at San Francisco University," Candice said.

Good thing I didn't say where I went to college.

"What are you studying?" I asked.

"Chemistry."

I said, "Wow. That's impressive."

Double thank goodness I didn't say where I went to college - she could easily know Dee. I'll have to ask Dee if she knows Candice.

"How about you, Deirdre?" I asked.

"I'm a scientist. I work in biotech."

My eyes widened. "My gosh, two scientists at one table. That's amazing. I'm so jealous of your brains." And I was. Not that I hadn't done well in high school chemistry, but I had majored in business and investigations and avoided science in college.

Deirdre said, "It's not that big of a deal."

I said, "Nonsense. You should be proud of your accomplishments."

Reba said, "That's what I always tell them."

Ignoring the praise, Deirdre said, "You said you knew Stephanie and that she wasn't doing well?"

"That's right. We work together. She collapsed at home and then had to undergo open-heart surgery."

Deirdre gasped. "That's terrible."

"Yeah, she hasn't woken up from the surgery yet. The doctor said they may keep her under for a while so that she can heal. Her heart valves were in pretty poor condition."

The three women looked at each other.

"What is it?" I asked.

Deirdre said, "It's nothing, really. It's just..."

"It's just what?" I asked. I hoped not to be too pushy, but I had a feeling they had answers, and I wanted them.

"It's just that there have been a few other women who were in a group with us and doing the program, but they stopped showing up."

Stephanie wasn't the first. "What were their names?"

Deirdre said, "Kelly and Alex. I'm not sure of their last names."

"How long ago did they go missing?" I asked.

Deirdre clarified, "They weren't missing. They just stopped coming to the group."

"How long ago?" I asked.

Deirdre said, "It's been a few months."

There had to be a reason Deirdre brought up the two absentee women. Did she suspect something sinister? I made a mental note about Kelly and Alex. Somehow, I needed to find their records and then find them to see if they also had heart valve issues like Stephanie. "None of you ever followed up with Kelly or Alex to find out if they're okay?" I asked.

"We were told by Dr. Teeling that they'd fallen out of the program and that it wasn't good for our recovery to talk to them."

That was suspicious as heck. "Really?"

"It's what he said," Deirdre said, rather suspiciously.

"What's he like - Dr. Teeling?" I asked.

Reba said, "He's super cool. He really wants to help us."

I'm not sure I believed an unlicensed disgraced physician practicing medicine under a fake name really wanted to help anything other than his own bank account.

"Does he give you anything to help with your disorder? Like meds?" I asked, as casually as I could.

Candice and Reba looked at one another before Reba said, "He offers a vitamin supplement that he says can really help with weight loss. They're really expensive. But I've been on them for a month and a half and have lost thirty-five pounds."

My brows shot up. "You've lost thirty-five pounds in a month and a half?"

"Yeah, it's super awesome. I'm so glad I found Dr. Teeling."

Candice said, "I'm still saving up, but as soon as I have the money, I'm getting them, too."

I glanced over at Deirdre, who gave me a look as if she didn't approve.

I said, "Frieda never mentioned vitamins at my intake."

Deirdre said, "You have to be in the program for a little while before they let you have them, and we're not supposed to talk about them."

Suspicious much? "Why not?"

Reba said, "Dr. Teeling told me he wants us to lose weight - i.e. stop binging - on our own without vitamins, but sometimes when he has seen that we've done all we can by ourselves, he says the vitamins can help, like a little crutch. He says it's just a little fat burning fuel. Works like a charm."

Candice gazed out. "I'm so jealous."

"What kind of vitamins are they?" I asked.

"I don't know. He says they're some special blend that the Chinese have been using for centuries and that they're perfectly safe."

"Do you have them with you?" I asked.

Reba squished up her face. *Oops. I shouldn't have asked that.* Reba said, "No, I don't carry them around with me. Why?"

I tried to recover. "I'm just curious to see if maybe if I've seen them before."

"Have you taken diet pills before?" Reba asked.

After putting on my actor hat, I shrugged. "I've done it all to lose weight. I've tried making myself throw up - which I'm terrible at, so then I tried laxatives, and that was just painful, and then I tried the over-the-counter appetite suppressants. Nothing ever worked," I lied.

Reba said, "I have done all that, too. But if you stick with the program, I think you'll find that it's a safe place to help with your disorder. It's good to have people around who know what you're going through."

I said, "Thanks. I hope so."

We ordered a light lunch and continue to chat about non-weight loss related things. These women were amazing and so much more than their body type. When would the rest of the world catch up with that realization? And who were Kelly and Alex - and more importantly, what happened to them?

14

SELENA

After a thoroughly enjoyable lunch with Deirdre, Reba, and Candice, I strolled out to the parking lot toward my car. I was hoping to go back to the clinic and try to find out who the rest of the staff were. The man I spotted in the group session room seemed sketchy. *I knew sketchy.* And if I could locate the good doctor, I wanted to learn more about him - like why he hadn't shown up for work or if he was peddling illegal drugs to his patients. If he wasn't at the clinic, I would have to check on the address associated with his car registration. Maybe that was where he had been hiding out, or maybe he really had a family emergency. Only one way to find out.

A few steps from my car, I heard my name. I swung around and smiled. "Hi, Deirdre. What's up?"

Deirdre said, "I just wanted to talk to you about what we said in there."

"Oh, don't worry. I won't tell anybody what the three of you said."

"No, that's not what I meant. You were asking about drugs or diet pills that the clinic handed out."

I studied Deirdre's face. She was in her thirties and looked healthy. I was no doctor, but she wasn't someone I would have expected to have an eating disorder or be suicidal, but I guessed you really couldn't judge a book by its cover. But something about the look in her eyes said she was worried.

Deirdre continued, "I just wanted to warn you that if they offer you the pills, don't take them."

Now she had my attention. What did she know about the pills? "Why not? What's wrong with them?"

"Look, I don't know what they are, but like I told you, I'm a biochemist by training, so I just don't think they are safe. I want you to keep that in mind. They're not worth it."

That's right. Deirdre is a scientist. Maybe I should show her the pills I had found in Stephanie's apartment - but thought better of it. I didn't know Deirdre from any other stranger walking down the street. She seemed like a nice, decent person, but you never really knew. "Did you tell the others about your suspicions?"

"Yes, but they didn't listen. I think the pills could be really dangerous. Please don't take them."

Why would Deirdre still go to the clinic if she thought they were giving out dangerous drugs? "Why do you think the vitamins are dangerous? Have you tried them?"

"Look, I just know that the vitamins they give out - I don't think they are really vitamins."

"Have you tested them?" I asked.

Deirdre stepped back. "No, of course not. Nothing like that. I want to be thin and beautiful just like everybody else, but I don't think it's healthy to rely on, quote-unquote, vitamins. I wish Reba would listen to my concerns. But after I warned her, she told me she was willing to risk it. She said she had been dieting for so long and wanted to be thin so bad she would try anything - even if it wasn't healthy."

That was sad. Reba had seemed very excited that she had

lost those thirty-five pounds. But even I knew losing thirty-five pounds in a month and a half was insane - there was no way that the weight loss had been healthy. Reba's story sounded a lot like Stephanie's case. I said, "But Reba seems fine."

"Some people are fine. Some people aren't."

What else did Deirdre know? "Some people like Kelly and Alex? Do you know more about them? Did they have medical issues, and that's why they stopped going to the clinic?"

"Look, I can't... I don't really know. But I suspect they were having some side effects before they stopped coming. They both complained of feeling dizzy, but they weren't bothered by it because they were happy about losing weight and said if being dizzy was the side effect of the vitamins, so be it. They'd be a little dizzy."

"How long have you been going to the clinic?" I asked.

Deirdre leaned against the car in the parking lot. Was it her car? "Three months." She crossed her arms over her chest and had a stance that was strangely familiar. Something about her demeanor had me wanting to know more about Deirdre.

She glanced down and then back up at me. "How is Stephanie doing? Do the doctors think she'll make it?"

"She's not in good shape. She had to have open heart surgery because of some faulty heart valves. The family didn't know she had a heart condition, but her sister suspects it has something to do with her diet." I shouldn't say too much - I couldn't give away my cover.

"What does her sister suspect?" Deirdre asked.

"I'm not exactly sure. When I visited Stephanie in the hospital, her sister didn't say much other than she thought it was related to her dieting."

"Were you pretty close to Stephanie? I thought you said you only worked together for about a month."

Oops. *Right.* "She was really helpful when I first started at the company - we were fast friends. She was kind of like my mentor, and we were attached at the hip my first few weeks."

"Where did you say you were from?" Deirdre asked.

"San Diego."

"What part of San Diego?"

Was she interrogating me? "La Jolla." It was the only part of San Diego I knew of because I had applied to UC San Diego in my senior year of high school.

"So, you come from money?"

Deirdre sure was inquisitive.

I said, "No, I was down there for school."

"So, you're not from San Diego?"

She was definitely interrogating me. "I'm originally from the Bay Area."

"That makes sense. You had mentioned that you go to your dad and stepmom's house every Sunday night for dinner."

I had been undercover before but never like this - this was like deep cover. At that moment, with all of Deirdre's questions, I was feeling unprepared and a bit of an amateur. My previous undercover gigs were at a frat party and at a nail salon for a day, so my undercover story wasn't extensive. And here I was, forming relationships, having to keep up with a back story which was all fictional. This was going to be tougher than I had thought. "Are you from around here too?"

Deirdre nodded.

"Can I ask you a question?"

Deirdre said, "Sure."

"Can you remember the very first time in your life when you thought your appearance and being thin were the most impor-tant thing?"

Deirdre hesitated. "I can. I was bullied in high school by one girl - the head cheerleader. For some reason, she had picked on me and gave me the nickname of Fatty D. Before that, I never really considered myself to have body issues or thought that I needed to lose weight. I was an athlete and had always been strong. But those words and taunting by her and her cronies cut me deep." Deirdre's expression turned sad. Then again, she also tried to kill herself recently, so there was likely something bigger going on. "It was good talking to you, Selena. I hope to see you at the clinic."

"Wait a second."

"What is it?" Deirdre asked.

"You work in a lab, right?"

"Yes."

"Would you be able to test the vitamins in your lab, so we can figure out what's in them?"

Deirdre looked at me strangely and didn't speak right away. "I'm not sure how my employer would feel about that. I just wish the other women would stay away from them. But, despite all the counseling they've received, they still just want to be thin."

"Sounds like the clinic isn't helping anyone."

Deirdre shrugged. "I guess it depends on what you think help looks like."

How many people went to the clinic for the drugs to get skinny and how many of them were there to get well? "But you keep going to the clinic. Do you think it helps you? I mean, you're saying you won't take the pills, so the group counseling and one-on-one with Dr. Teeling must be effective, at least for you?"

Straight-faced, she said, "I like being around a group of people with a similar disorder, even if most of them are just there to get the drugs to be skinny. You know, if you don't feel comfortable at this clinic, there are other places you can go to get real help."

Real help? What did Deirdre really know? Was there something she wasn't telling me? "Well, thanks for that. You know, you're really easy to talk to. Maybe we can get together after a session and grab a coffee."

Deirdre nodded. "I'd like that. What's your number? I'll put it in my phone."

After exchanging phone numbers, I waved and smiled. Something was very intriguing about Deirdre. It was like she knew something more, but she wouldn't tell me what. If I got closer to her and went a little deeper undercover, she might tell me everything she knew, and then I could get to the bottom of what was really going on at the Teeling's Clinic.

15

STEPHANIE, AGE 19

PRACTICALLY LAUGHING OUR HEADS OFF, VICKI AND I
entered the dining room of our parents' house. None of the
guests had arrived yet, but I suspected Grandma must be
around somewhere - considering I smelled her famous pumpkin
pie. Oh, how I loved pumpkin pie with a giant dollop of
whipped cream on top. But who was I kidding? I loved everything about Thanksgiving. The turkey, the mashed potatoes,
and the rolls with butter and gravy - not to mention the home-
made stuffing my mother made every year. Yes, Thanksgiving
was definitely my favorite holiday. Not just because of the food
but because it was when the family got together. It wasn't full of
greed and stress like the other big holidays. It was our tradition
that every year we said what we were thankful for before we
started in on dinner.

It was my first time coming home from college, and I felt like
a changed person. I had only been out in the world, on my own,
for three months, but I felt older, more mature, and ready to sit
at the adults' table at Thanksgiving. Rounding the corner, I
spotted Grandma coming out of the kitchen. *I knew it. I'd know
the smell of Grandma's pie anywhere.*

Grandma threw her hands in the air. "My girls." She embraced me and gave me a big bear hug like she did every time we saw each other, and then she did the same with Vicki. Grandma stepped back and looked at the two of us. "My goodness. You two are the most beautiful young women I've ever seen. How have you been? I want to hear everything."

Vicki said, "I love my new job," and described to Grandma everything about it, including the few cute guys in the office.

Vicki was five years older than me and had started working at her first job after graduating from college the previous spring. Vicki was one of the best sisters I'd ever known. She was my only sister, but compared to my friends and people I had met in college - I found out that Vicki and I were the closest siblings. She wasn't just my sister, she was my best friend.

Grandma turned to look at me. "How is college? Have you got a new boyfriend yet?"

My smile disappeared. "Nobody serious."

A month after graduation, Bill had come out of the closet. He was gay. To say it shocked me was an understatement. We broke up after that, considering I was the wrong gender. Were the only good ones really gay or married? I had met no new prospects at college, but it hadn't been a priority. I had been going to parties and having a great time with my roommates while living in a dorm. It was a party almost every single night, which was super fun and so different from how I had been raised. I felt free and was having the time of my life. "How are your classes?"

"They're great. I love them."

"Have you decided on a major yet?"

"I'm leaning toward communications or business or psychology or..."

Vicki nudged me. "Don't worry, sis. You don't have to declare until your third year anyway, right?"

"That's true. I have time to figure it all out." And I would. I did not know what I would be when I grew up and graduated from college and figured maybe I would take Vicki's advice and not worry about it for the time being. I was nineteen and living my life to the fullest. I had plenty of time to figure out what I would do with my life.

Grandma said, "Well, it's so good to see you girls."

"We're so happy to see you too, Grandma. And I'm excited for your pie too. I could smell it when we walked in."

She looked me up and down and smiled. "Maybe just a little slice this year. It looks like you gained the freshman fifteen."

Her words stung my very core.

I glanced down at my stomach and looked over at Vicki, who shrugged with a grimace. Grandma was known for being blunt, but that was uncalled for. We were having such a good time. Why did she feel the need to point out my weight? Had I really gained that much?

"What have you been doing, Grandma?" Vicki asked.

I could tell Vicki was attempting to distract Grandma from picking apart my self-esteem any further. Maybe I was having too much fun at college. It was true I hadn't worried about calories or carbs since I'd arrived in the dorm. Nobody else seemed to be concerned. Well, not really, anyway. Sure, there were the bulimics and anorexics, but they existed in high school too, so that wasn't anything new. My roommates didn't care about calories or if they were eating too many cookies or drinking too much soda and booze. They were great roommates. I felt so comfortable with them and could be myself.

Maybe I'd gotten too comfortable. As Grandma told Vicki about her bingo games and a cruise she just booked with her single lady friends, I quietly excused myself to go to the bathroom. I shut the door behind me and locked it. Staring in the mirror, I looked for the signs that I had gained weight. Shaking my head back and forth, I stripped off my clothes and shut my eyes before stepping on the scale.

After a deep breath, I opened my eyes and stared at the numbers on the scale. I had not gained the freshman fifteen, my gosh, I had gained the freshman twenty. Was that a thing? How had I put on that much weight in such a short amount of time?

I stepped off the scale and quickly put my clothes back on. Refocused on my reflection in the mirror, I looked myself in the eyes and said, "You can have Thanksgiving dinner, but the diet starts tomorrow."

THE NEXT MORNING, I WOKE UP IN MY OLD BED AND glanced around the room. It was time to start my new diet. This time, I was going to stick to it. There would be no more comments about my weight from Grandma or anyone else. Still in my pajamas, I walked out to the living room and was met by Mom, who was cheerfully making a cup of coffee. "Morning, honey."

"Morning, Mom."

The sound of slippers dragging on the carpet behind me caused me to turn around. I spotted my favorite ally. "Morning, Vicki. How did you sleep?"

Vicki said, "Like a baby. Is there coffee?"

Mom said, "It's just about ready."

"What are you making for breakfast? Pancakes, waffles?" Vicki asked.

I shook my head. "Oh, no, not for me. My diet starts today."

Mom tapped me on the shoulder. "Nonsense, honey. You're home. I'll make you your favorite - chocolate chip pancakes. What do you say?"

She knew I couldn't resist chocolate chip pancakes. She

probably had leftover whipped cream, too. "Okay, pancakes it is."

After a sugar filled breakfast and lots of fun catching up with Vicki, I snuck back into the bathroom at the far end of the house and turned on the fan. Standing over the toilet, I said to myself, "You can do this." I crouched down on my knees with one hand on the toilet seat rim. I shoved a finger down my throat and then pulled it out. Nothing. I needed to poke farther to activate my gag reflex - it hadn't even been triggered a little. I tried again - this time much farther down my throat - and heaved and gagged. But no vomit. I never had much of a gag reflex and rarely threw up throughout my life. I rarely got food poisoning and didn't get sick that often either. Maybe bulimia wasn't for me? How did those other girls make it look so easy?

I heard some girls in the bathroom at school talking about taking laxatives. That seemed easy enough - all you had to do was take a pill, right? It would be significantly better than having to count calories.

That was one thing I admired about all the women I'd met who were bulimic - they didn't have to be obsessed about calories or entering every bite they took into an app on their phone. They could eat as much as they wanted and then just threw it up like it never happened. Unfortunately, I thought my future as a bulimic was out of the question.

Laxatives - now that was something I could get on board with. I shut the toilet lid and rifled through the medicine cabinet. No laxatives. I would have to go to the store later and buy them with nobody noticing. Maybe it would have to wait until I got back to school. There, I wouldn't have anybody breathing down my neck. Waiting a few more days wouldn't make that big of a difference anyway. On my drive back to school, I would stop for a few groceries plus laxatives. Yes, that could definitely work.

16

SELENA

AFTER DRIVING DOWN EVERY AISLE OF THE PARKING LOT AT the clinic, there was no sign of Dr. Teeling's car. Where was he? I supposed it was time to check out his home address. I was about to pull out of the parking lot when I spotted the man I'd seen the day before talking to Reba in the group therapy session room. He was tall and gangly, with greasy hair. He didn't look like somebody you would expect to work in a medical facility. I watched as he got into the driver's side of a green pickup truck. *Hmm. Perhaps I will learn more about this particular man.* I quickly recorded his license plate number in my phone and followed him out of the parking lot. I didn't even know his first name, but I was sure I could follow up with Reba and ask her about him.

As I continued to follow the man, I thought back to my conversation with Deirdre. There was something going on there, but I wasn't sure what. At least I had her phone number, so I could search the databases to see who was attached to her account. The truth was, I didn't fully trust her. Her story about being worried about the so-called vitamins, yet continuing to go to the clinic for three months, wasn't adding up for me. But she had the heart-wrenching story in the group about her suicide attempt. Maybe I was looking further into my conversation with Deirdre than I needed to - but just in case, I'd run her phone number to learn more about her before attempting to become allies with her.

It was early enough in the afternoon that there wasn't much traffic on the highway, and the man in the truck didn't seem to be concerned about somebody following him. Other than his high speed, he wasn't difficult to follow. Ten minutes into the pursuit, I realized this would be a longer journey than I had expected, and, after forty minutes passed, it was clear we were headed in the same direction Dr. Teeling had gone the day before. What was out on there in the far East Bay?

I needed to be smarter about my pursuit this time and couldn't be spotted or lost. Keeping my distance, but also monitoring the man in the truck, I begged the universe the man wouldn't pull into that same gas station. If he did, maybe there was something significant about the gas station? Sailing past the gas station, I continued to follow the truck into a residential area filled with dilapidated homes. There wasn't a green lawn in sight. The truck turned left onto a side street before pulling into the driveway of a white house with paint peeling down the sides and a few other old trucks in the driveway.

I drove past, making a left around the corner so I wouldn't be seen. Down the street, I pulled over and parked my car. Reaching over the center console, I opened my glove box and grabbed my black hat and sunglasses. Fitted with my disguise, I studied the house I had parked in front of. There weren't any lights on and no cars in the drive. Likely, there wasn't anybody home. That was lucky. I didn't need anyone coming out and telling me not to park in front of their house.

Out of the car, I trudged toward the end of the street and turned to the right to get a better look at what surrounded the white house. Assessing the area, I figured I could probably duck behind a set of bushes and watch the house for a while. Reaching the hedge, I crouched down and peeked through. To my surprise, the man was still in the driveway, fiddling with his phone. When he was done, he didn't go into the main house but into a large barn-type garage behind the primary home. A workshop maybe?

From my back pocket, I slipped out my phone and entered the license plate numbers of the other two trucks in the driveway, as well as the address on the front of the house. Pointing my camera phone up at the street sign, I snapped a picture and then took another set of snapshots of the house and garage - the entire scene.

A few minutes later, the man from the clinic emerged from the back garage with a large brown paper bag in his arms. He opened his truck door and climbed in. I took another quick photo and knelt back down. The engine on the truck roared, and he backed out of the driveway and headed toward the road in which we came in. Was he going back to the clinic, or somewhere else?

For another ten minutes, I watched the house and garage but didn't see anybody come in or out. After calling it quits, I headed back to my car. A woman in the house next door to the white house stepped out onto her porch and gave me a quizzical look. Hurrying my steps to get out of there as quickly as I could, I turned down the street my car was parked on. With my car in my sight, I froze.

A man I had never seen before leaned on the hood of my car. Out of instinct, I reached into the interior pocket of my jacket and grabbed my baton before proceeding toward the stranger who had taken up residence on my vehicle. Who the heck was he? Was he waiting for me or simply hanging out?

17

SELENA

APPROACHING THE CAR SLOWLY, I STUDIED THE MAN. HE wore a long-sleeved black fleece, blue jeans, black-and-white sneakers, a navy blue baseball cap, and a pair of aviator sunglasses. He was kind of dressed like - me. With my baton in hand, I was ready to push the button to extend it to its full size in the event this man attacked me or things turned violent. Body tense, I stared at him and said, "You're on my car."

"Sorry about that." He pushed off and stood in front of me.

Triggering my baton to full-length, I was ready for a fight.

He smirked. "No need for that. I'm not going to hurt you."

Said every predator ever. I said, "I'll be the judge of that. What are you doing on my car?"

"I wanted for us to have a chat."

"Who are you?"

"That isn't something you need to be concerned about. What I'd like to know is who you are and what you're doing here."

Was he one of Dr. Teeling's goons? Did the man in the truck know I had followed him and signaled this guy?

"My name is Selena. What's yours?"

"You can call me Hank."

"All right, Hank. I'm a very busy woman, and I need to get going. So, bye." I continued to my driver side, with the baton ready for a confrontation. The man was much larger than I was and could probably take me out if he had a weapon.

"Selena, I just wanted to talk. There is no reason to rush away."

Stepping back, I said, "Okay. Talk."

"Here's what I need from you. I need you to stay away from that house. Do you think you can do that?"

Why did he want me to stay away from the house? Was there something illegal going on there? "Why should I?"

"You seem like a really nice lady. I'd hate for something bad to happen to you."

Hand on my hip, I said, "I can take care of myself. What's it to you, anyway?"

"Stay away - so you don't get hurt."

"Is that a threat?" I didn't like being threatened and really didn't like being threatened by some guy who was sitting on my car in the middle of frickin' Brentwood.

"If you know what's good for you, you will stay away." And with that, he walked down the street and disappeared out of view.

What the heck was that about?

18

STEPHANIE, AGE 21

RUMMAGING THROUGH JANINE'S CLOSET, I PULLED OUT THE hanger with a black miniskirt dangling from it. "I love this one." Janine said, "You should wear it. Try it on."

"Are you sure?"

"Yeah. If it fits, go for it."

I said, "Thanks."

Janine had been living in Seattle since high school graduation. She went to the University of Washington while I had stayed in California. Tammy and I had decided to take a road trip for a weekend visit. We had been friends since as far back as I could remember. It was so good to see the two of them and to have the three of us back together again. Even though we hadn't hung out since high school, it was as if no time had passed at all.

One reason Janine, Tammy, and I had gotten together was because it was Janine's twenty-first birthday. The three of us were all now of legal age, and we could drink and party and live it up. Tonight, we were going clubbing, and it was going to be epic.

I slipped on the skirt and said to Janine, "How does it look?"

"It looks great. Who would've thought you and I would be the same size?" She chuckled.

A pit formed in my stomach. "Funny, right?"

Janine and Tammy had always been thin without dieting. I was always the odd man out, carrying an extra twenty pounds. Not anymore. Sadness filled me. Why? It wasn't a secret she'd always been thin, and I hadn't been. Maybe I'd thought I'd always been overly insecure about my weight, but obviously Janine had noticed that I was bigger. Why else would she say such a thing? Why was she surprised she and I would wear the same size? Like I couldn't do it? I couldn't stick to a diet? Well, I had.

I shook off the thought. I had been really good and counted every calorie and went to bed hungry most nights. If my stomach growled as I lay down my head, I knew I had triumphed. After all these years of dieting, I'd nearly met my goal weight. The skirt I was wearing was a size six. I had never been a size six - not even when I was a kid.

I slipped on the top I had brought from home and walked over to the full-length mirror to stand next to Janine. After smoothing down the skirt, I flipped my hair over. I looked pretty good - definitely thinner than I had ever been before. I stared at my thighs, exposed by the miniskirt. They were smaller, but I could probably still lose five pounds. My stomach rumbled. I would have to ignore the hunger pains tonight; I couldn't afford calories for food and cocktails, so I had to choose. I chose cocktails. After all, it was Janine's twenty-first birthday.

What was that quote from that one supermodel? "Nothing tastes better than how skinny feels." Something like that. She was right. I loved being thin. Or thinner, at least. The journey wasn't easy since I wasn't lucky enough to have the willpower to be anorexic or the gag reflex of the bulimics. My first year of college, I had tried laxatives. That didn't go very well either.

After the first time I took them, my stomach hurt so bad I gave up on the idea. Since then, I had counted every calorie that I put into my mouth and entered them into the app on my phone. It had all paid off, and now Janine and I were the same size. I was finally normal. Of course, I still had room to improve. I could lose another five pounds, and I would. No pain, no gain, right?

19

SELENA

With my mind spinning from the encounter back in the far East Bay city of Brentwood, I hurried from the parking lot, looking in all directions to see if they had followed me. It didn't appear so. I unlocked the door to my office, went inside, and locked it behind me. During normal business hours, I typically kept the door unlocked so that if someone just happened by and needed a private investigator, bam, there I was. But with too many strange things I didn't understand happening, I decided I didn't need any new clients until I had my current investigation under control. I didn't like being rattled or surprised. Come to think of it, I had never liked surprises. Not when I was a kid, not as a teen, and certainly not when investigating a case.

The more I thought about it, the more I thought that somebody had to have been following me. Maybe the man in the navy blue baseball cap who warned me to stay away from that white house with the barn garage in the back was following me - but when? Who else would have known I was there? What was going on, and how had this simple case of finding out what kind of drug Stephanie had taken become so incredibly bizarre? What had I stumbled into?

Setting down my backpack, I opened the mini fridge, helping myself to a bottled water. The drinks were usually reserved for clients, since I carried my own refillable water bottle, but I had been so nervous during my drive back that I drained mine. After unscrewing the cap while watching the front door, I gulped down the entire bottle of water.

This was a time when, if I were still at Drakos Monroe Security & Investigations, I would've marched into Martina's office and talked over everything that had happened. We would have discussed different approaches and plausible scenarios for what was going on. Martina was a great sounding board. Truthfully, I wasn't used to working on my own, at least not all the time. In my previous investigations, I didn't exactly have a partner, but I always had someone to talk the case through with. Like when I had investigated the frat house where Dee was sexually assaulted. Dee and I had discussed the plans, and then eventually, when things were especially dangerous, Martina provided some input that helped to take down the bad guys. Same thing when I was investigating the disappearance of a five-year-old girl but then ended up stumbling into a human trafficking ring. Martina always had my back. I was realizing how lonely this job could really be. Had I made the right decision to go out on my own?

What if Dr. Teeling's operation was more dangerous than I had calculated? Maybe *he* was dangerous. Maybe they were manufacturing the drugs themselves? What if they came after me? I didn't have any backup. I tried to think about what Martina would say if she were sitting across from me. I'd probably ask her what I should do, and then she'd answer my question with a question. She'd probably say something like, "Selena, ask yourself, is it worth it? Is the investigation worth losing your life or others'?" *Ugh.* Should I back out of the case? Should I just sit around and wait to find out what the drugs were and close out the case? I wasn't one to back down from a challenge, and I didn't think I could start now.

My nerves slightly calmer and my body hydrated, I turned on my computer to find out who that truck was registered to, as well as look into the property records for the white house in Brentwood. Maybe I'd find out the identity of the man in the navy blue baseball cap? As I was logging into the database, my cell phone rang. I answered the unknown caller and said, "Hello, this is Selena Bailey."

"Hello, Ms. Bailey. My name is Scott from the Bay Area Analytical Testing Lab."

Yes! The lab results from the pills found in the vitamin bottles at Stephanie's apartment could be some good news - an additional lead to help me with the investigation. "Great. I've been waiting for your call. Were you able to determine what the two pills are?"

"Yes, I'll email over the lab reports, but we could identify each of the compounds in the pills. The capsule we identified as phentermine, and the tablet is fenfluramine hydrochloride."

Great! So helpful. I do not know what any of that means. I hadn't heard of either of those and didn't know if they were dangerous. "Do you know what the drugs do?"

The man started to talk but then hesitated. "You haven't heard of Fen-Phen?"

Fen-Phen? "No, I'm sorry, but I'm not familiar with those drugs."

He said, "These drugs, the fenfluramine and dexfenfluramine, were banned by the FDA in the late 1990s. It was used in combination with the phentermine as a weight loss drug. When combined, they were given the common name of Fen-Phen. Fenfluramine and dexfenfluramine are essentially the same drug and were found to cause valvular disease and pulmonary hypertension - both conditions are potentially fatal."

Valvular disease? Like Stephanie had. "Wow. So, if you say the FDA banned this fenfluramine, then do you know how someone could get it?"

"I'm no expert, but they could only buy it illegally."

"Is it easy to make?" I asked.

"Honestly, I'm not sure. I just test it and was around in the nineties when the story was on every news channel. It started with one woman who died after using the drugs for only three or four weeks. She was trying to fit into her wedding dress. She died a few months later from taking Fen-Phen."

Did the woman who died from Fen-Phen not care that she might have been taking a potentially fatal drug just to look slim on her wedding day? "While the people were getting sick and dying from Fen-Phen, did they know the drugs were dangerous? The women who took it, I mean."

"That's the thing. From what I understand, they didn't know. The news reported that after people who took the drugs were getting seriously ill, some dying, that the drug companies and even some members of the FDA were very familiar with the risks and understood the potential side effects of using the drugs. It was revealed that the drug caused severe valvular disease and pulmonary hypertension. It was found out when doctors from across the country started seeing that their patients were having these odd symptoms and connected them to Fen-Phen. Those doctors brought the issues to light and eventually got fenfluramine off the market so that doctors could no longer prescribe it to people trying to lose weight."

The FDA knew it was bad for people? Weren't they supposed to be protecting the public? And the drug companies knew? I couldn't believe it. "They knew it was unsafe, but they sold it anyway, and the FDA approved it?" I shook my head. "I'm sorry to keep you. I'm just surprised, and you seem to know a lot about the situation, and to be honest, in the nineties, I was far too young to know about any of this."

"May I ask how you got the pills you submitted?"

"I'm a private investigator, and I found them in the possession of one of my client's family members. That family member has had to undergo open heart surgery because of some strange valve issues she was having."

The man on the line snickered. "Well, you can call your client and let them know exactly why their family member had to have open heart surgery and valve repair. If she took Fen-Phen, it was the Fen-Phen. I'm guessing she is a young woman?"

"Yes."

"Well, I hope she survives. And best of luck to you."

"Thanks. I'll let the family know right away."

"You have a good day, Ms. Bailey."

"You too." I ended the call and thought about what I had learned. Somebody was giving potentially lethal drugs to unsuspecting victims - like Reba and Candice. If this somebody was Dr. Teeling, I would take him down. But, if the FDA had banned fenfluramine, was Dr. Teeling getting it from a drug company that was still selling it secretly to clinics? Or did Teeling's goons cook the drugs themselves? Either way, I needed to let Vicki know right away that we may have found the cause of her sister's severe illness. However, before I called, I did a quick internet search to learn more about this Fen-Phen - more specifically fenfluramine, which sounded like it was the most likely cause of the heart problems Stephanie had experienced.

Retreating from the computer monitor, I was disturbed by what I had learned. Like the man from the testing lab had said, according to the news reports, the drug companies knowingly marketed and sold their drug to women and men - anyone desperate to lose weight. To be perfect. To be flawless. To date, the drug companies had paid over $5 billion in lawsuits. Even so, in some cases, the money paid out to the victims barely covered medical expenses. And that didn't even account for the number of women who lost their lives, just by taking drugs the companies knew were unsafe, that some people even at the FDA knew were unsafe. How did it all get started? Who came up with the idea that men and women need to look a certain way to be loved? Who had decided what was normal? The more I continued to read, the more horrified I became.

Some articles even went as far as saying that they thought the entire obesity epidemic was created by the pharmaceutical companies trying to sell the idea to the American public that it would be safer to take drugs than to be twenty pounds 'overweight' and by doing so making billions from them as well as the weight loss industry as a whole. Obesity Inc. is what some reporters called the phenomenon. So, while some people lost their lives and some had to live with long-term illnesses, others, like the diet industry, were racking up billions in profits? As I read more, my mouth dropped open. The weight loss and diet industry was valued at more than $100 billion. If the diet industry was truly helping people and trying to improve the health of the American people, then why were Americans larger than ever?

My heart pounded as sadness and rage were all rolled into one ball in my being.

So much heartache and so much sadness, for what? *Money.*

After drinking another bottle of water to calm my nerves, I called Vicki Crawford. I needed to present a professional demeanor and not the outraged young woman I was. She picked up after one ring. "Hi, Vicki. This is Selena."

"Hi, Selena."

"How is Stephanie doing? Has she woken up yet?" I asked.

"She has. She opened her eyes, and she squeezed my hand

and my mom's. She's not totally there yet. The doctors say she has a lot of healing to do. Not just from the surgery but from whatever she'd been taking before. They're hopeful she will recover, but it's going to be a long road."

"That's good to hear. I have some news on that front. I just spoke with the lab. Stephanie had been taking what was commonly known as Fen-Phen - a combination of phentermine and fenfluramine for weight loss."

"Fen-Phen?" Vicki asked.

"Have you heard of it?" Had everybody heard of it except for me? Was I the last female not obsessed with weight loss or getting the quote-unquote 'perfect body?'

Vicki said, "Yes. It has deadly side effects."

"You should definitely tell her doctors. The lab technician I spoke with told me a little about it, and I looked it up online, too. It sounds like the heart valve issues Stephanie has could be a direct correlation to taking the fenfluramine, which was banned by the FDA back in the nineties."

"That's right - my gosh."

I didn't tell her that some of the articles I found said some of the people who took the drug continued to have side effects even ten to twenty years after stopping them. "I've read it's really important that you tell the doctors because maybe she could develop other issues from using the drugs as well. Things that maybe haven't shown up yet."

The sound of sniffles emitted from my cellphone speaker. I knew this wasn't exactly good news, but it was some news. "I'll tell the doctors right away. Thank you, Selena."

I had identified the drugs, and Stephanie seemed to be on the mend, at least for now anyway. Was the case closed? I had a feeling I was just hitting the surface of what was really going on at the Teeling's Clinic.

"Now that we know what the drugs are and Stephanie

seems to be on the mend, do you want me to continue to look into the clinic and how Stephanie got a hold of the drugs, or is this enough for your family right now? I would totally understand if you wanted to put this to rest. I'm sure Stephanie's health is the number one priority."

Vicki's breathing was heavy, as if exasperated. She responded, "If you can, Selena, I want you to figure out where she got those drugs, who gave them to her, and I want them exposed. I want them in jail. Will you help me do that?"

"Yes. I will absolutely do that." I'd had a feeling Vicki wanted me to continue to investigate, but I wanted to make sure. It could get very expensive for her and time-consuming for me. I continued, "There have been a few developments, but maybe you and I can meet in a few days once I have some concrete information to share with you. How does that sound?"

"That sounds good. I'll let my parents know. Whatever it costs, we want people to pay for what they've done to my sister and god only knows who else."

"Got it. Take care, and tell your parents I said hello and that I'm thinking positive thoughts for your whole family."

I ended the call with a little disbelief at how big this case had become. Considering the extent of Stephanie's injuries, it made sense. It wouldn't be a quick open and shut case. There was definitely criminal activity going on. The first being the dispensing of illegal drugs to unsuspecting people who had sought help with an eating disorder. The Teeling's Clinic website stated it helped heal those with eating disorders, but it was obviously a front for an illegal weight loss pill mill. Now I just needed to prove it and find out exactly who was involved and therefore responsible for Stephanie's condition.

20

SELENA

FINDING THE NAME AND ADDRESS OF THE REGISTERED owner of the truck filled me with a sense of determination. I shoved all the supplies I would need into my backpack. It was going to be a long night. After zipping it shut, I slipped my arm through the arm strap, but before I could charge out of the office, my cell phone buzzed on the table. "Hi, Martina. What's up?"

"Hi, Selena. How are you?"

"I'm good." *Sort of.*

"I was calling because I was hoping to change our Sunday night dinner to Saturday night if you can make it?"

"Sure. I'm open on Saturday." My social life wasn't exactly a party every night. I graduated a semester early and even when I was in school, I hadn't been much of a partier, but it meant that all the friends I'd met in college, like Dee, were still in school and studying hard in their last semester.

"That's great to hear. Zoey is coming home on Saturday but has to leave Sunday morning, and I thought it would be great for all four of us to have dinner together."

"Awesome. She didn't tell me she was coming home. Is it a last-minute thing?"

"Yes, she said she got a last-minute project at UC Davis and she wanted to stop by and see us on the way."

Zoey was my stepsister and currently studying veterinary medicine in Oregon. We didn't get to see each other much, but we emailed all the time and texted too. We were only a year apart, but our personalities were quite different. Zoey was bubbly and happy and optimistic - like all the time. She also loved animals and was super smart. "What time is dinner on Saturday night?"

"I was hoping you could come over early, like four. We can have appetizers first and catch up."

"Sounds great."

"How is your case going?" Martina asked.

How is it going? I was on my own - the lone employee - and I had a lot on my plate. Not to mention I was still a bit rattled by just about every part of the case - the Fen-Phen scandal, the man in the navy blue ball cap, and the fact that all the people at the clinic taking the drugs may be in danger. "It has had some developments..." I explained everything I had learned but left out the part about the man in the navy blue cap.

"That's incredible that you could get that much information so quickly. It sounds like you've found yourself in the midst of a dangerous case. If they're pushing illegal drugs, that means there are drug dealers involved. Drug dealers don't tend to be very nice people. Well, sometimes they're nice enough people, but when you cross them, they do what they have to do. They aren't afraid of violence."

Martina was right. Even I understood it was a dangerous situation, but Vicki had hired me to do a job and that job was what I would do. I hadn't pursued my conceal and carry license yet - since it was more difficult to get in California than I had expected. Plus, I hadn't spent much time at the gun range, although I should have. My baton was my only weapon other than my self-defense training.

Training differed from real-world situations, and I wondered if my training would be adequate. It had been a long time since I've done a case that was so big. I realized, in that moment, how big this case actually was. I was trying to bust an illegal drug operation in the Bay Area - alone. Trying to conceal my uneasiness, I said, "I suspect it might be. I'm being extra cautious, especially after what happened today."

"What else happened today?"

I pondered how much to tell Martina because I wasn't in the mood for a lecture about safety or being on the lookout, but I did like the idea of Martina giving me her take on things. "I followed one worker from the clinic to a house out in Brentwood where he went in and exited the back garage with a bag in hand."

"That may be where they're making the drugs, or it could be a stash house," Martina added.

"Yeah, that's what I suspect, too. But that's not really the bad part or it may be, but when I got back to my car, which I had parked around the corner, there was a man sitting on the hood. He threatened me. He told me to stay away if I knew what was good for me."

Silence from Martina. She wasn't one to be quiet, especially when she had an opinion, and she never shied away from telling me what she thought, or if she thought something was off, or if I was being stupid. She never used the word stupid, but foolish may have been thrown around a time or two. In hindsight, she was probably right.

When she finally spoke, she said, "Selena, I don't think I need to tell you that this could be a very, very dangerous situation for you, and I don't want to preach, but you're a one person operation. You don't have backup. And as somebody who cares deeply about you, I have to say I think you should back away from this. Bring your suspicions to the local police department and tell them what you found."

It hadn't even occurred to me to go to the police with what I'd found - not yet, anyway. I didn't have any evidence that Stephanie had gotten the pills from the clinic. "It's something for me to consider, I suppose."

"I think you should definitely consider it. No job is worth dying over."

"I agree. I just haven't linked the clinic to the drugs yet. Once I can, I can bring that to the police, and then I can wash my hands of it."

"How do you plan to make that connection? If the person who was hanging around your car is working for the clinic to supply the drugs and they know you, your cover may be compromised. You may not be able to go back to the clinic safely."

I hadn't considered that. If that man was working for Teeling, then they could have notified the clinic and plan to nab me when I walked in. And do what - kill me? Maybe they'd just try to scare me a little? I wasn't convinced my cover was blown yet, but I would tread carefully. "You're right. I'm gonna have to think about this more."

"You know that if anything goes sideways or something doesn't look right, you can call me anytime, right?" she asked.

I tried not to do that. I didn't work for Martina anymore. It didn't seem right that I would continue to go back to her and use up Drakos Monroe's resources.

"I appreciate that. If I think I'm in danger, I'll let you know."

"You know, maybe it's a good idea for you to text me your location when you go on a stakeout - just in case - especially if you think you're going to be in a potentially dangerous situation."

I knew that was the safe and smart thing to do. It was protocol at Drakos Monroe Security & Investigations, the firm that Martina was half owner of with her partner Stavros Drakos. I didn't have a partner, and I didn't have somebody to check in with. It was a smart idea. "Okay, I will."

"Great. I will see you on Saturday night. Selena - be safe."

"Thanks, I will."

Martina said, "I love you."

"I love you, too." I hung up the phone with some of the wind out of my sails. After packing up for the night thinking that I was going to stake out Teeling's Clinic and maybe break in to get information about the drugs or other important information about their operation, I decided to put the plan on ice.

Maybe I needed to take a different approach. Deirdre seemed to know a lot about what was going on and had her own suspicions. Did she know Jake Ruger - the man the truck was registered to and who, based on employment records, worked at Teeling's Clinic? Maybe she wasn't telling me everything she knew. There was only one way to find out.

21

SELENA

EQUIPPED WITH A NEW PLAN, I SET MY BACKPACK DOWN and fired up my computer. I needed to meet with Deirdre and find out what else she knew, but I also needed to know more about Deirdre. Could she be trusted? I'd learned I shouldn't trust anybody until I checked them out first. Deirdre was hiding something - I could feel it in my gut. But what? Was she in on the whole thing? Was she the drug maker? She was a biochemist, so it could fit. Or was she, like, a double agent type they used to determine who they could trust to be given the drugs?

Logged into the database, I entered the phone number Deirdre gave me and then let the computer do its thing. I was probably being overcautious, but overcautious was better than blowing an entire investigation. This was my first actual case under Bailey Investigations, and I didn't want to get a poor reputation for not delivering on my client's needs.

I tilted my head as if that would make the search results on the screen any different. It was strange and certainly not what I had expected. There were no records. It was a burner phone. Drug dealers and criminals or people who didn't want to be traced or people with bad credit or people who didn't trust cell phone companies typically used burner phones. Did Deirdre fit into one of those categories?

Deirdre claimed she was a scientist. Maybe she was but didn't want to give out her actual phone number? Maybe she did top secret work. Even if any of that was true, something wasn't sitting right with me. All signs were pointing to the fact Deirdre was hiding something and knew more than she let on.

I didn't even know her last name - or much about her, really. She said she had major depression and binge eating disorder, but then she had a burner phone and had suspicions about the vitamins. I had a feeling she was closer to this than I had originally thought. I needed to hide those suspicions so that I could befriend Deirdre to get on the inside track.

The clock showed it was getting late but not too late for a phone call. After I dialed Deirdre's burner phone, it rang three times before she answered. "Hello."

"Hi, is this Deirdre?"

"Yes."

"Hi, this is Selena. We met at the clinic."

"Oh, hi, Selena. How are you?"

I said, "I'm doing all right, mostly. I'm sorry if this is forward, reaching out like this, but I've been backsliding, and part of me is feeling anxious. I'm outside the grocery store and want to go in and buy every cookie on the shelf and then go to the frozen food aisle and buy up all the Ben & Jerry's. I was just hoping maybe you and I could talk."

She paused and then said, "Can you hold on for a second? Let me check something."

It was 5:30 PM on a Friday. I was hoping she was available to meet me for dinner or coffee or something. But if she couldn't, maybe I'd suggest to meet the next day. All I could do was hope at this point. But if I could get a license plate number for Deirdre, I could figure out who she really was.

Deirdre returned to the line. "Hi, Selena. If you can, we could meet at the local coffee shop, get some tea. How does that sound?"

Yes. Feeling lucky now. "Sounds great."

"All right. I'll text you the details, and I'll meet you there."

"Great."

"Stay strong, Selena. We can talk you through this."

The call filled me with mixed emotions. If Deirdre was part of the drug dealing operation, would she have agreed to meet with me to make sure I didn't binge eat? Maybe. Was she a drug dealer with a heart of gold? Maybe she was being forced to make drugs for them. Maybe she was actually a wonderful person but somehow, they were blackmailing her into doing their dirty work. Maybe she was crying out to me for help. Maybe she wanted out of the operation. There were so many possible scenarios. I just needed to know more.

22

SELENA

WITH A LONG FACE, I OPENED THE DOOR TO THE COFFEE shop. I wasn't sad or anxious, but I needed to look that way. Surely, I could draw from my experience to play the role. It was almost as if it was the role I was born to play. Isn't that something? Inside the coffee house, my nostrils were filled with the scent of freshly ground coffee beans. Hello, coffee, my old friend - and drug of choice.

It was a rather large café. There were many people reading books or on laptops busy in their own world, drinking coffee and eating baked goods. I spotted Deirdre in the far corner and raised my hand to wave before pointing at the register to indicate I was going to order a cup of tea. It was a bit late for coffee. Martina said green tea was supposed to be good for me - I'd give it a shot. Order complete, I grabbed the table number and headed toward Deirdre. Taking the seat across from her, I said, "Thank you so much for meeting with me."

"No problem. So, do you want to tell me what you're feeling anxious about?" Deirdre asked.

On the way over, I had created my story. Being undercover this time was much more difficult than I had experienced in the past. This was an ongoing persona I need to keep up. Lesson learned. Next time, I would put together a solid dossier with all my undercover history, wants, desires, and needs - a full character profile. I said, "It's my dad."

"What about your dad?" Deirdre asked with concern.

That feeling that I was betraying a good person settled within me again. Deirdre seemed genuinely concerned about me. "Well, I just found out he has a heart condition, and the idea of losing him sends me down a spiral. He's my only biological parent left and I just - it's got me rattled, you know?"

Deirdre nodded. "The thought of losing a parent is really troubling. I can understand why you'd be feeling anxious. You said you had a therapist before. Did the two of you come up with a plan to help deal with your anxiety?"

Of course we did. "Yes, I usually turn to exercise. Running or going to the gym. But I already went to the gym today, and I know I shouldn't be over-exercising. I really kind of struggle with what to do if I can't exercise to ease my anxiety. It's where I have the biggest weakness in my plan. I still haven't met with Dr. Teeling one-on-one, so I haven't had an individual session with a therapist in a while."

I watched Deirdre's face to see if my story was believable or not. She tipped her chin, as if contemplating everything I had told her. She said, "It is strange that Dr. Teeling didn't show up the last two days, but once he's available, I'm sure you'll be able to see him."

"Do you know a lot about the staff at the clinic?" I asked before I lifted my hands from the table so the server could put down the pot of hot water and a cup with a tea bag sitting next to it. I tore open the paper and set the sachet inside the cup and poured the hot steaming water over it. It would steep for a while, and then I could sip it - it would give me something to do with my hands and fill the voids so that she would talk more than I did.

As I got situated with my tea, I noticed Deirdre didn't answer my question. Was that intentional, or was she simply pausing because the server had been here? I repeated my question, "Yeah, so I was just wondering. You said you've been at the clinic for a few months. How well do you know the staff? I noticed there were a couple of group leaders and a man in scrubs I saw talking to Reba when I first came in. Is he a doctor too? I think Reba said his name was Jake?"

Deirdre didn't answer. Instead, she glanced around the room. There had to be thirty other people surrounding us. She said, "Maybe we should go somewhere else. Somewhere more private."

I wasn't sure how I felt about that. Yes, I did. I didn't like it, not one bit. Who was this woman, and why did we need to go somewhere more private?

"But I've got my tea. You can't just tell me more about Jake?"

She stared at me long enough that it caused a hint of fear inside of me. Something wasn't right. My heart pounded, and I wondered if I was in over my head. Maybe she was in on it and planning to take me somewhere to have me killed. Or worse. I didn't know what was worse. *That's not true.* Kidnapping and torture were pretty bad. Been there, done that. No thanks. Deirdre tipped her head and in a low voice said, "I know who you really are."

23

SELENA

WHAT DID SHE MEAN SHE KNEW WAS WHO I WAS? I WASN'T sure how dumb to play - only one way to find out. "I'm Selena. We've met before."

"Your name isn't Selena Jones," she said in the same hushed tone as before.

That's what she meant about knowing who I was, or at least who I wasn't.

She continued, "I don't know what you're doing at the clinic. I don't know if you really have an eating disorder, and if you do, I'd like to help you. I can refer you to somebody else, not Dr. Teeling. You can't go back to the clinic - not until you meet privately with me."

Was she threatening me too? I sat there, stunned, not sure how to respond. How did she know who I was? How did she know who I was, but I didn't know who she was? I didn't like that. "Who are you really? Are you in on it? Are you the cook?" I asked.

She shushed me. "Keep your voice down."

I suddenly felt very ill-equipped for the mission and wished I had told Martina where I was going. This could end badly, very badly — like dead badly. I glanced around, looking at the different exits. I should've known better than to meet someone who I knew nothing about. It was a pretty public place, and I had my car, so it wasn't totally stupid, I guess.

Deirdre continued to study me. She said, "Don't leave. There's a conference room in the back. It's down the hall on the left, and then you make another right. The coffee shop rents them out for study groups. Meet me there in ten minutes."

She got up and exited the café without waiting for my reply.

Was now the time to text Martina? Although if I texted Martina using my phone, what if my phone was being traced or something? Had I been compromised, like Martina suggested?

What would happen at the back of the coffee shop? She wouldn't kill me in such a public place. I hoped. Uneasiness filled my gut, but I knew what I had to do. While sipping my tea, I texted Martina my location and then waited for the time to pass.

Now empty, I brought my used dishes over to the dish bin above the garbage bins. I glanced around the coffee shop once more before heading back to the small room where Deirdre had asked me to meet her.

Before I entered the room, I took a selfie. All my photos backed up to the cloud, so if this was the last place I was to be seen alive, at least there would be a record. Assuming this turned sinister, these people wouldn't get away with it.

After a deep breath, I lifted my chin and headed toward the back room. There was no window on the door. I didn't like that. I knocked lightly. A man's voice responded, "Come in."

Heart racing, I turned the knob and stepped one foot inside. My heart nearly stopped at the sight of the man - wearing a navy blue baseball cap.

Why was he here - and how did he know Deirdre? They were both in on it. Deirdre said, "It's okay, Selena, come on in."

I turned to the right, where Deirdre leaned against the wall. The scene was familiar. Oddly familiar. I walked inside and shut the door behind me.

The man said, "Why don't you have a seat, Ms. Selena Bailey, private investigator."

Okay, they know who I am. "I prefer to stand. What's going on? Who are you? Who are you really?" I demanded, more confidently than I actually felt.

"My name is Agent Dan Mundy. You've met my associate, Deirdre, also known as Agent Deirdre Long."

Deirdre, or Agent Long, or whatever her name was, said, "I'm with the DEA. Mundy's FBI. We have been staking out the clinic, and I think you know why."

"Because they're selling illegal drugs to women who want to lose weight?" I asked.

Mundy said, "Bingo. We can't have you compromising our operation."

I stepped back, a little shocked that I had stumbled into a joint FBI and DEA operation. "How long have you been looking into Dr. Teeling?" I asked.

"Three months. Like I told you at lunch, two women went missing - actually they died - Alex and Kelly. Stephanie's the third to get seriously ill since we began our operation at Teeling's. We moved in when we started getting reports that fenfluramine was back on the streets. They sent me undercover to infiltrate the clinic. We were pretty close to taking them down, and then you walked smack dab in the middle of it."

"So, you know they're giving out dangerous drugs. Can you prove it?" I asked.

Deirdre said, "Not yet."

"How are you going to do it? Can't you just simply ask one of the women to testify that they got the drugs from him?" I asked.

"They're all sworn to secrecy and more concerned about staying thin than putting him away. They think he's a miracle doctor. Trust me, I've been trying for months to convince them that whatever drugs he's giving them, it's not good. They swear up and down they're not getting any drugs and that they're vitamins. They're not vitamins, but we haven't been able to get a hold of them yet."

I had something they didn't. "I have some."

"What? How?" Agent Mundy asked.

"Stephanie's sister hired me to find out what happened to her. That's why I started going to the clinic. I don't actually have an eating disorder — it's my cover. When I searched Stephanie's apartment, I found a couple of vitamin bottles with strange looking tablets inside. I sent them to a lab to be tested. They are Fen-Phen."

The two agents looked at each other. "Would you testify to that?" Deirdre asked.

I shrugged. "Sure, I can testify that I found them in Stephanie's apartment, but you can't prove that she got them at the clinic, right?" I held a degree in criminal justice and knew the law.

Agent Mundy sighed. "You're right, we can't. We need to prove it. We're hoping you can help us."

"How so?" I asked. Even though I had a feeling I knew what it was.

Deirdre said, "I haven't been successful at getting my hands on the pills, and those other women won't give them up, but if you could convince one of them, then maybe we could nail him and put him away for good."

"Is that necessary? I mean, Dr. Teeling is practicing medicine without a license. Can't you arrest him for that?" I asked.

"We could, but we don't want the doctor to get away with a fine and a slap on the wrist. We want him to go away for a long time, and we don't want just him. We want to take down the entire drug operation. We think it might be bigger than just Fen-Phen. We think Teeling is actually just a small fish in a much bigger pond."

I restrained from rolling my eyes. I'd heard this scenario before. The little fish tended to get away with things so that the big fish was on the hook. I didn't like it. I didn't like it when it happened with the human traffickers who killed my boyfriend, and I didn't like that the big fish got away with it too. How many people needed to die to bring the Teeling operation down?

"So, what? You want me to continue to be undercover and work with you guys?"

Deirdre said, "Yes."

"But there're rules," Agent Mundy said.

"Rules?" I asked.

Mundy said, "It's a confidential investigation. You can't tell anybody about it, and you have to check in with us every step of the way."

Deirdre said, "It'll be dangerous."

I insisted, "I can take care of myself."

Agent Mundy smirked.

I said, "I could have taken you out if I wanted to," with probably a little more sass than was necessary or enough to make me credible. Truth was I may have been in trouble if I'd had to spar with him. Thankfully, he'd been an agent and not one of the bad guys. "Is that why you have a burner phone?" I asked Deirdre.

"You ran my number?" she asked.

I nodded.

"It's for the operation. Will you help us?" Deirdre asked.

It was an excellent opportunity, but I couldn't do this while telling no one. More specifically, I couldn't do it without telling Martina. I said, "On one condition. We bring in my stepmother - just on an intelligence basis. She's also a private investigator."

Deirdre said, "We know who Martina Monroe is and her reputation. As long as she agrees to the confidentiality, the two of you can openly discuss the case."

"You both will need to sign some documents before we get started," Agent Mundy added.

"I'll talk to Martina and get back to you." What would Martina say? Would she tell me I needed to quit? That I needed to put my safety ahead of the operation?

Working with the FBI and the DEA - this case may be the biggest one of my career. It would be kind of cool to work with law enforcement, and I definitely wanted to. I just hoped Martina would be onboard with it. Obviously, it was my decision, but it would make me feel better if Martina supported it.

24

STEPHANIE, AGE 22

FINALLY, I WAS DONE WITH COLLEGE AND READY TO START the rest of my life. The last semester had been rough. I'd had to take an extra class to make sure I graduated on time, but I did it. I passed all my classes. Graduation day was a blast. Mom and Dad and Vicki were there along with Grandma and a few aunts and uncles and the odd cousin. I was proud of myself - I had accomplished a lot. I was a college graduate. Woot. And I even landed my first job - I started a week from Monday. Double woot.

The day was amazing. Smiles and champagne and cake and pictures. I grabbed my phone from the nightstand and scrolled through the photos that we had taken. The number of black caps and gowns was dizzying. I scrolled back to the very beginning of the day to watch and replay one of the best days of my entire life - giddy to see how it was captured forever in my photo stream.

The first photos I took were of Vicki and Mom, who stood close together with wide smiles. I continued to scroll and stopped on the photo with Vicki and me. I was in my cap and gown - I frowned. I looked like a burnt marshmallow. I continued to scroll to the after party, where I had shed my cap and gown to wear my party clothes.

Wearing a silver-sparkle mini dress, I smiled widely, but now my smile was long gone. As I studied each photo of myself more closely, I saw that my thighs were huge. My arms were flabby. From the side, my belly looked pregnant. The overall look said disco ball on holiday. How had I not realized it until that moment?

Filled with humiliation, I wondered if everybody had seen how awful I looked and were just too nice to say anything.

The last few months of finishing up school, all I did was study. That meant skipping the gym, and counting calories wasn't something I had in my capacity. And it showed. I must've gained...

Throwing my phone back down on the bed, I ran into my parents' bathroom and stripped down to my birthday suit and stepped on the scale. Eyes wide, I felt sick. I had gained ten pounds. Ten hard fought pounds. I had been so good until that last semester. It was hard to lose ten pounds - so hard - and they came back without me even noticing them.

I redressed with the sinking feeling that I had failed once again. Sure, I could get a college degree, but I didn't have the control to make sure I didn't gain ten pounds? What was wrong with me?

How could I accomplish so many things but couldn't stick to a regular diet and not be flabby and pudgy and looking like a disco ball? Was I that weak?

No wonder I hadn't dated at all this last semester. Men didn't like fat women, right? Next week, the family was leaving for a Hawaiian vacation - a celebration of my graduation. How could I put on a bathing suit now? Not that I didn't belong in the water with the other whales. Nope, I would be the beached variety, covered up to hide the fact I couldn't control my body or what I ate. Why couldn't I be like other women who didn't shove food into their face every time they got a chance or like those who didn't hate their bodies or themselves for having no self-control?

Why couldn't I just be normal - and thin?

25

SELENA

WITH A SMILE PLASTERED ON MY FACE, I APPROACHED Mrs. Pearson. Her eyes lit up, and her fuchsia lips curled up into a smile. As I waved, she lifted from her seat and hurried around the desk to embrace me in a warm hug. She smelled like lilacs, which I expected most grandmothers would smell like. After a very long squeeze, Mrs. Pearson stepped back. "Selena, dear, it's so good to see you. How are you?"

Mrs. Pearson was the receptionist at Drakos Monroe Security & Investigations, where I had worked part time for the last three and a half years. From what I understood from Martina, Mrs. Pearson had been employee number one after Stavros Drakos. She looked like a grandma, but she was more like a secret assassin who knew everything that went on in the office. Nothing got past Mrs. Pearson. "I'm doing great."

"How is your first week as Selena Bailey, PI? You know, we're so proud of you around here."

"It's been eventful."

"Oh, do you have your first challenging case already?"

"I do, and to be honest, it's bigger than I expected, much

bigger. That's why I'm here to see Martina. I need to talk to her about it."

"Does she know you're coming?"

"She does. I phoned her before I came in. She said she was in a meeting but that she could meet me soon." It was convenient that Martina's office was so close to mine – which, when she and Dad had gifted me the lease, Martina had pointed out, saying we could have lunch and discuss cases if I wanted to.

"Well, dear, make yourself comfortable back there. You know where Martina's office is. I know I don't have to show you," she said with a chuckle.

"Thanks, Mrs. Pearson."

"You take care, dear."

"You too." I continued back into the familiar gray cubicle world that I used to live in when I was at Drakos Monroe. It was where I had learned everything about private investigations; it was practically a college education in itself. They were the toughest, smartest group of people I had ever met. Martina and Stavros only hired the best of the best — and me. I had simply lucked out because Martina was my stepmother. It wasn't the norm for an eighteen-year-old to get her foot in the door of an operation such as Drakos Monroe and then get shown the ropes while being able to get the required hours to get my PI license at age twenty-one. I learned a lot during my time at Drakos Monroe, but I wasn't naïve enough to think I didn't have a lot more to learn. Never having worked with the feds or the police before, I couldn't imagine going into something like that without having Martina as a sounding board.

This week, I'd contemplated whether I was leaning on her too much. After all, I was an independent PI, yet I'd talked to her several times, and it was only week one. When I reached Martina's office, the door was closed. She'd probably had a busy day, it being the end of the week and all. Through the glass window of her office, I could tell that she was on the phone, but she was by herself. Waving in front of the window, I smiled and waited for her to be available.

Since I had graduated from college, I hadn't come back into the office, and I was feeling some nostalgia. Drakos Monroe Security & Investigations would always be a part of me. The team was like a family, and I was treated like I was everybody's daughter. It was nice in one way and a little suffocating in another. I didn't enjoy being the newbie, the one who knew the least amount about everything.

Martina hung up the phone and got up to open the door. "Come on in, Selena."

"Hi. Thanks for seeing me last minute."

Martina had left her door open, but I closed it quietly behind me. Her eyes met mine, and she gave me a look that acknowledged this was a serious conversation. I sat down across from her, and she studied me for a moment and then asked, "What's going on? Has Stephanie's case turned dangerous?"

"It's gotten to be a lot more than that..." I explained the FBI and DEA involvement and their request for me to go under-cover and work with them.

Martina sat back in her chair as she seemed to absorb every-thing I had told her.

"What do you think? Should I do it?" I asked.

She was taking her time responding. In the past, Martina had explained that she bordered on being overprotective with me but also knew she and I were a lot alike, so she tried to balance her motherly nature with my personality.

"Well, I have additional questions. It could still be very dangerous for you, but in some ways, I'm glad you have the backup of the FBI and the DEA, which means they'll probably have you mic'd up most of the time. So, I guess, if something went bad, they could be there in a flash to make sure nothing *terrible* happened to you. That doesn't mean there's no risk. If the investigation is that big, it means there's probably a lot of risk."

"Have you ever worked with law enforcement before - like the DEA or the FBI or the police? How does it work as a civilian?"

Martina smiled, as if remembering something fondly. "I have. I don't think I ever told you this, but for a while, Stavros and I weren't seeing eye to eye on a lot of things. This was about ten years ago, and I ended up being contracted to the CoCo County Sheriff's Department to work alongside a detective in the cold case division."

I had no idea. "You're kidding?"

"No. Do you remember meeting my friend Hirsch, or August, as my mom calls him, at your dad and my wedding?"

"I think so. He kind of looks like a Ken doll?"

Martina laughed. "Yes. He was the detective I worked with."

What else about Martina didn't I know? Probably a lot. "Oh. I assumed he had worked at the firm."

"Nope. He was a homicide detective before leading the cold case squad. He and I didn't always get along, but once we did, we were great partners."

"That's fascinating. Sometime, I'd love to hear more about that."

Martina said, "One day."

"So, then, you know what it's like to work with law enforcement."

"I do. It can be tricky. It's a situation where you have to follow all the rules, which I know can be tricky for some people." She raised her brows at me.

I know, I know. Point taken. I didn't like to follow the rules if they made little sense or if ignoring them could help me solve a case or put the bad guys in prison. "Well, I understand that aspect, and they told me I had to agree to confidentiality and sign paperwork and everything. I told them I couldn't agree without talking to you first and being able to discuss the case with you. They agreed I could bring you in. You'd also have to sign some paperwork."

She nodded. "If this is something you really want to do, I will support you. I'll sign whatever documentation they need so you and I can talk things over as the case unfolds. For example, if you have questions you don't feel comfortable speaking to the DEA or FBI about or you just want to discuss your role - PI to PI."

I had hoped that's what Martina would say and that she wouldn't talk me out of it because I was secretly pretty excited about the whole thing. When I was in college before I went the private investigator route, I had contemplated going into law enforcement. Martina had a lot of contacts at the police department who told me I could easily go either way. I opted for private investigations, thinking that maybe sometimes the rules were too hard to follow. But I was excited to get a first-hand glimpse into a DEA investigation. Even if I remained a PI forever, it would be a great experience and a real resume builder in the event I wanted to go work for another firm and not stay out on my own. I said, "Great."

"I'm guessing you're looking forward to it?" Martin asked.

I nodded.

Martina said, "I'm glad you felt comfortable coming to me and that you wanted me to be in on this too, so we can discuss it. It means a lot to me, Selena."

I said, "I appreciate that you're always there for me."

Oh boy, how did discussions with Martina always lead to me practically tearing up in her office? I was a tough private investigator, yet Martina turned me emotional most of the time. I think it was because Martina was the mother anybody would want. She was fair; she was tough. She was a role model and the most caring person I'd ever met. Not to mention how happy she made Dad. He really hit the jackpot when he met her.

Even with having the best stepmother in the world, which I was pretty sure was accurate, I still missed my mom. Sometimes I thought about how, if she had lived through to my adulthood, I could've helped her get out of the cycle of having to rely on men, and she could have gotten her life together. She could have been happy and sober, but of course, her jerky boyfriend took that option away. I shook off the thoughts - I needed to be focused on the investigation.

26

SELENA

Standing as still as I could, I tried to distract myself from what was happening. A male technician, who I hadn't met until five minutes before, was fastening wires to a mic on my chest. I didn't like standing so exposed in front of people I didn't know - especially not a man.

He said, "Just breathe."

My nerves must be showing more than I had thought. As excited as I was to be working with law enforcement, I was anxious. It was one thing to be undercover with nobody watching your every move. It was quite another with a team monitoring every word you said and every step you made. I won't lie. I have made mistakes - big mistakes, and I felt like the operation was in my hands. *No pressure.* All I had to do was prove that Teeling and Jake were in on the drug dealing together and tie them to the clinic so law enforcement would have enough to prosecute. No sweat. Okay, maybe a little sweat.

He said, "That'll do it. You can put your shirt on now."

I whispered, "Thank you," before grabbing my shirt from the chair next to where I stood.

We had gone over the operation details over the past few

days - including beefing up my back story so I didn't blow the entire operation. I didn't blame them. I'd screwed things up before and had to make sure I didn't do it again. During our preparation meetings, I had been told what to ask and what to say with only minimal input from me - I was told not to take it personally. There was something about being around the seasoned agents that made me feel like I was out of my depth. *Fake it till you make it.* It was time for me to go face-to-face with Dr. Teeling a.k.a. Douglas Potter, and the team didn't think we would have too many shots at him.

The past few days, I barely slept, which didn't make things any easier. There was a little relaxation Saturday night when I went to Martina and Dad's for dinner. It was so good to see Zoey, who was the most outgoing, cheerful, bubbly person I had ever met. She was excited to be working on some research at the veterinary school at UC Davis. I was glad to hear she would come back through the Bay Area the following weekend, so we could meet up again. There was even talk of maybe going to a movie and out to dinner like normal people. *I only have to survive the week and then normalcy, at least for a night, will be mine.*

When I approached the table where Deirdre and Mundy were sitting, Deirdre asked, "Are you ready?"

"I'm ready. Let's do this."

"Great. Is there anything else you need before heading over to the clinic?" Deirdre asked.

"Nope." I waved and headed out the back door of the café toward my car. They had me mic'd up and a GPS tracker attached to my car. The GPS tracker was Martina's idea. All eyes and ears were on me. It made me feel safe and a little creeped out at the same time.

EXTENDING MY HAND TO SHAKE DR. TEELING'S, MY confidence grew. This man didn't know who I was. This man wouldn't see through my cover.

"Please have a seat."

I nodded and sat in the chair across from Dr. Teeling's desk. He said, "I read through the notes from your intake with Freida. It says here that you have attended one of our group sessions. How did that go? Do you think that is something you would like to continue to attend?"

"Yes, it's nice to be part of a group that knows what I'm going through. I feel like BED is such a misunderstood disease, you know. It's a tough one, because we don't all look alike. All sizes and shapes. So, it's hard to find people like me."

"You're very right, Selena. It says here that you went to lunch with some of the other participants too - that must have been nice."

How did he know that? "Yes, it was so nice to meet new people. People who struggle like me."

"It says here that you also know Stephanie Crawford."

I had been in therapy for years, and so I knew this conversation was very odd. How did he know I knew Stephanie? And who had put in my file that I had gone to lunch with Reba, Candice, and Deirdre? "Yes. Stephanie's a coworker of mine."

One woman from that lunch must have reported back to someone about it. Who? Obviously not Deirdre - but was it Reba or Candice? Dr. Teeling said, "I hear Stephanie's not doing that well but that she came out of surgery and is expected to make it."

"Yes, it's good news."

"Do the doctors have any idea what caused her issues?"

I hadn't expected him to ask me about Stephanie or my lunch with those women. Thinking quick on my feet, I said,

"Someone at the office said they thought she had a heart condition she didn't know about. Genetics, I think."

"I'm glad they got to her in time."

This guy is totes suspish. "Me too."

"With the group counseling, do you feel you need the one-on-one therapy as well?"

"Yeah, I think that would be really helpful. My old therapist was good at helping me when I was kinda stuck. You know, when I was about to fall backwards."

"I understand."

I continued, "And sometimes I feel like I'm spinning out of control. You know? The new job, new friends, and new clinic have me a bit off balance. I'm afraid I'm going to binge and gain weight. It's so hard to lose the pounds once I've stacked them on. How does the clinic help with weight loss after a slip up?"

"Well, we think the cognitive-behavioral therapy can be quite effective. Like us, talking right now. We'd be able to talk you through what's troubling you the most and determine some coping strategies."

"That sounds great."

"Back to what you were saying earlier about feeling anxious about starting a new job. Do you want to talk more about that?" Dr. Teeling asked.

No. "I just started my new job and the first one since college, and I feel like maybe everybody knows more than I do, you know? I'm at the bottom of the totem pole, and I worry maybe I'll never be as good as the rest of them."

"Are there other parts of your life where you also feel you'll never measure up?"

Maybe. "Yes, I tend to compare myself to other people, especially with my appearance. I hate being fatter than other people. It makes me think I'm less in control. Before Stephanie collapsed, she told me you had special vitamins that could help me in case I backtracked. Is that something you have, in case I need them?"

Dr. Teeling removed his glasses and raked his fingers through his silver hair. It was an odd gesture for a therapist. To me, it said he was having to think about this far too much. He either had something to give me or he didn't. If what he was doing was on the up and up, it wouldn't be something he needed to contemplate, right? He refocused on me and said, "We recommend that all of our patients take a multivitamin to make sure you are getting all the nutrients that you need. That must be what Stephanie was referring to."

Interesting. Did he not believe my story? Why wouldn't he give me the pills? "Oh, that must be it. I guess I thought maybe there was something more, but what you're saying is you just recommend a regular multivitamin I can buy at the grocery store?"

"That's right. Now, like the receptionist mentioned, this is just the consultation to see if you and I are a good fit. I could refer you to another doctor if you don't think so. My schedule is pretty booked, but I might be able to start one-on-one sessions as early as two weeks from tomorrow. Does that work for you? In the meantime, you can attend as many group sessions as you'd like. We offer them several days a week."

I nodded. "I'd like that." *I won't have access to him for another two weeks?*

"If you have any other questions, please don't hesitate to ask Freida. And there's another group session starting in about twenty minutes if you want to attend."

"Thanks, Dr. Teeling."

A.k.a Dr. Fraud.

As I exited his office, I sensed the doctor didn't trust me at all, which was why he had told me he only recommended multivitamins to his patients. If he was giving out the deadly pills, he wasn't handing them out willy-nilly. I needed to chat up Jake - the man in the truck that I had followed.

Headed toward the group therapy session room, I was hoping to catch a glimpse of him again. As I entered the room, sure enough, he was over in the corner with Reba again. Was Reba the rat, giving intel on all the new patients to see if they were trustworthy enough to get the pills? Was that why she was so cozy with Jake?

I waved as I walked in, trying to be as friendly as possible. "Hi, Reba. How are you?"

She broke away from her chat with Jake and headed over. "I'm great. You?"

"Taking it one day at a time." I stared over at Jake, who was watching me intently. And then I looked at Reba. "Who is this?" I asked in a flirtatious manner. Jake wasn't totally awful looking but certainly not my type. I wasn't into slimy criminals or drug dealers.

Reba said, "This is Jake. You haven't met yet?"

"No." I extended my hand. "Hi, I'm Selena, nice to meet you."

He grabbed my hand and shook it gently while caressing my palm with his index finger. *Gross.* "It's very nice to meet you, Selena."

I suppressed the urge to do a massive eye roll. Taking my hand back, I checked to make sure it wasn't now covered in slime or mold or whatever this guy was oozing. "I heard that Jake here is the guy who knows how to get things."

He flinched at the suggestion. But then relaxed his body. "I can definitely get you what you want. Meet me after the session. Out in the parking lot. I have to run an errand. You can come with me."

"Okay," I said with a flirty smile.

I watched him walk out of the room with a bit of a swagger. *Ick.* I refocused on Reba. "He seems nice."

"How did you know?" Reba asked.

"Know what?"

Reba said, "That Jake can get things."

"Oh, that. I was just guessing. Hoping. Don't tell anyone, okay?"

Reba narrowed her gaze. "Guessing? You must know something."

"Stephanie told me there were some vitamins that were really good, and she told me before her collapse that there was someone here who would get them for me. Dr. Teeling didn't seem to want to give me any, so I assumed it was Jake."

Reba looked me up and down. "Okay."

I didn't know if she bought it, but at least I had a meeting with Jake. Maybe he would lead me to the drugs and, if I was lucky, his supplier.

After the session, I stood up, wiping a tear from my eye. This week, I shared a story - a fake story - and I played it beautifully. Tears and all. As I was getting up to leave, Deirdre tapped me on the shoulder. "Hey, Selena, can I talk to you for a second?" Her tone was cheerful and not like she was a secret DEA agent.

"What is it?" I asked.

She lowered her voice. "The feds told me about your conversation. Don't meet with Jake. I don't think it's safe."

Had they texted her? How did she know? "Why not?"

"We need to tie Teeling and Jake to the drugs. Not just Jake."

"But if we get Jake on tape giving me drugs, we'll be one step closer. Maybe he'll flip on Teeling. I'll be fine."

Worry spread across her face. "Fine. We'll follow close

behind. For the record, I don't think it's a good idea, but we've got your back."

"Yes. A latté sounds great," I said, louder than I was speaking before to make it look like we were having a normal conversation and not plotting an undercover operation. Adrenaline pumping, I headed out to the parking lot, ready to bust these guys.

27

SELENA

SHOULDERS BACK AND HEAD HELD HIGH, I STRUTTED OUT to the parking lot. I immediately spotted Jake leaning against his truck. It was time to turn on my feminine wiles. It was almost as if my honey trap was using their own game against them. The men who decided that women should be beautiful and thin and tall and look a certain way — were too silly to realize that same facade would end up as a weapon to be used against them. It was like they created their own monster. *Men.* I approached with a wide smile. "Hey, Jake."

He returned a gremlin-like smile. "Hey. We can take my truck."

Ick. "I definitely like the idea of going for a ride." *Double-ick.* That was even a little too gross for me.

He opened the door, and I cooed. "What a gentleman."

I hopped in and fastened my seatbelt. The truck was dirty, with garbage on the floor. He was a total slob. He got inside and turned on the truck. I eyed him and asked, "Where are we going?"

"Just running an errand."

"A work errand?"

"Don't worry. I'll get you what you want."

"Cool. So, how long have you worked at the clinic?"

Without looking over at me, he answered, "A few years."

Vague much? "Do you get along well with Dr. Teeling? I just met him for the first time today."

Jake smirked. "He's a chump."

I hadn't expected that. "Not a fan?"

"Yeah, he's a piece of work, but he'll do whatever I ask him to. Don't worry, if he gives you any trouble, just let me know."

Were we wrong about who was in charge? "He takes orders from you. How does that work?"

"I know some things about the doctor, and now he does what we ask."

We? "Oh, he's not like a creeper or something, right?"

"Nothing like that. But if you need anything, just let me know."

"Cool." Although Teeling was practicing medicine without a license, maybe he wasn't the mastermind behind the drugs after all. Maybe that was why he didn't offer them to me? "I'm really glad you're able to help me out. I just need to get to my goal weight, and I'm not far off. Just another ten pounds."

He gave me the side eye. "You ladies and your diets. From where I'm sitting, you look pretty perfect. I, for one, would surely like a taste."

Ick. "You're so sweet."

He pulled into a residential neighborhood that I wasn't familiar with and parked in front of a light blue house with terra-cotta roof tiles. "Wait here. I'll be right back."

"Okay."

I sat tight while I watched him hop out of the truck and hurry to the front door. He pulled keys from his pocket and unlocked the door and went in, shutting the door behind him. I didn't think it would be wise to hop out and try to see what was happening inside. It was unknown whether he'd be gone for a minute or thirty minutes. Although I sure would like to get an idea of what was happening in there, but it wasn't worth the risk. I glanced over at the street sign and said, "I'm at 7134 Bronson Street."

Tapping my fingers on the seat, I thought about how I kind of liked this wired up operation. Everything was being recorded, so I needed to get him talking more about the operation. I thought he'd open up if I stroked his ego a little.

The door reopened, and Jake hurried out, carrying a brown paper bag in his hands. He locked up behind him and jogged toward the truck, climbing in rather quickly and slamming the door. He turned to face me. "Okay, I've got the vitamins. How many do you need?"

"Well, I need to lose about ten pounds. I think Stephanie said I probably needed about a month's supply?"

He pulled out two plastic baggies from the sack - one with capsules and the other with tablets. He handed them to me. "Here you go."

I grinned and shoved them in my backpack.

"So, you know Stephanie? How is she?" he asked.

"She all right. She's in the hospital, actually."

"Yeah, I heard - bummer."

"So, these vitamins - do you know what's in them?" I asked as innocently as I could.

"Just some stuff - it's perfectly legal-ish," he said with a laugh.

"Oh, yeah, where do you get them? Are they from China?" I asked.

"Nope, we make them right here in the Bay Area. Not here. Not in this house, but I got some friends who make them. Don't worry, it's perfectly safe. Just, you know, don't tell anybody about it because if I told you I'd have to kill you." He laughed at his own joke.

Assuming it was a joke. I hoped it was a joke. "Don't worry, I won't utter another word about this."

"That's good." He licked his lips.

Ick. "Actually, since it's just you and me here. Can I make a confession?" I asked.

"I'm all ears, baby."

"I kind of have this thing for dealers. I know it's weird, but something about the risk and the secrecy turns me on."

"Oh, really?" he asked skeptically.

I pouted and said, "Yeah, like, would you let me see where your friend cooks it up? I'd be very grateful."

"I'm down for a little tit for tat. You show me yours, and I'll show you mine."

I gave a coy smile. "I feel like it's the other way around. You show me yours, and I'll show you mine."

His eyes turned dark. "Or I'll just take what I want."

It was clear his flirting was over, and he was about to try to take something that he would not get. "I'd like to go now. Thank you for the pills, and I'll see you at the clinic."

"No, honey, nothing comes for free. I gave you the pills. Now you give me what I want."

"Which is?"

"I want some of that sweet body of yours."

I shook my head. "No, thanks. I have cash. I'll pay for them. How much?"

"What are you, some kind of tease?"

"Hey, I'm just getting what I want. I'll give you some money for the pills. I'm not the kind of person who just goes in a stranger's truck and fools around."

"Oh, I think you're exactly that kind of girl. I see the tattoos and the piercings. You're exactly that girl."

There was that stereotyping again to come back and bite him in the ass. He moved his hand to my thigh, and I knew I had to get out of there. "I'd like to go now."

"Not so fast." He grabbed my other hip as I fumbled for the door, trying to escape. I elbowed him in the jaw, and he flew back but rebounded quickly. I lifted my boot and kicked him in the chest. He grabbed my ankle and started pulling me down, my back on the bench seat. He held me down and wrapped his hand around my neck as I kicked and clawed. He was stronger, much stronger than I had expected.

I pulled my baton from the front pocket of my backpack. The truck was cramped, and I wasn't sure I'd be able to extend it to full length. I opened it halfway and whacked him on the side of the head, knocking him off me. Then I kicked him in the chest again, pulled the door handle, and pushed open the door. Scrambling away from him, I grabbed the strap on my backpack, darted out of the truck - and ran.

28

STEPHANIE, AGE 25

SITTING AT MY DESK, MY SKIRT WAS CUTTING INTO MY belly like a knife. I would've chosen to wear something else, but everything else was equally tight fitting. I had obviously gained weight, and the scale confirmed it. When would I ever get this under control? I was twenty-five years old, and I really would have thought I would have figured this out by now. It was like I had been on a never-ending roller coaster of up and down, up and down. Recently, I had been reading online about body positivity and how I should love my body as it was. That sounded great in theory, but reality was a different story.

Sure, we were all different shapes and sizes, and that was good. Variety was the spice of life. And when I saw women who weren't stick thin, I didn't judge them. Honestly, when I saw a bigger person, I felt sorry for them. I knew they were probably struggling with their body like I had been for as long as I could remember. I knew what it was like to wish you were in a different body. I knew there were people of all sizes who loved themselves. Why couldn't I?

I tried to be less concerned about my weight and not count every calorie. All that did was make me balloon up. My clothes were too small, and I felt horrible about myself. How was I supposed to love my body when I had hated it most of my life?

Part of me wanted to give up - quit the fight. Maybe I was incapable of being thin. I'd read diet books from high protein to high fat to vegan to South Beach, and I had joined Weight Watchers the year before, only to gain every single pound back, plus a few. I felt like I'd done all the things there were to do, yet I was sitting there in clothing that was like a prison I couldn't get out of.

Maybe I had a thyroid problem? Something was definitely wrong with me. Or was I just too weak? Why couldn't I control my eating? After a bad day, I'd go to my cupboards and eat everything I could. It was like somebody else took over, and I had no control over what I put in my mouth. It was like this hungry monster lived inside of me, and I couldn't fight it until I had consumed everything in my house.

Even when I made sure there were no cookies, crackers, carbs, ice cream, basically nothing good in the house when that monster resurfaced, I either ordered pizza or went to the store and filled up. All to feed the monster. Mind over matter. I needed to focus on work and not food.

Returning my attention to my inbox, I read the new information regarding the employee orientations to be scheduled and benefit packages that needed to be compiled. No problem. Moving to the next message, the title made me pause. It was that time of year. The annual weight loss challenge at work. In previous years, I had passed on the competition, too afraid to step on a scale in front of a coworker. I didn't think I could handle the humiliation. I was about to delete the email when Karen came up to my cubicle. "Hey, girl."

"Hey. How's it going?"

"Good. Did you see the email about the weight loss challenge?"

I nodded. "I just saw it." Karen was one of my favorite office friends. She was all about the happy hours and periodic extended lunches. It was nice to have a good friend in the office, and I was lucky to have coworkers who were all about the same age and liked to do the same things like traveling, watching movies, and dancing.

"Well, I'm thinking about joining, and I think we can win."

"What do you mean?"

"You know how I told you I was going to a new doctor's office?" Karen asked.

"Sure."

Karen stepped back and twirled around. "I've been taking his vitamins for the last three weeks. I'm down twenty pounds."

My jaw dropped as I studied her frame. She looked thinner. "Seriously?"

Karen said, "Yeah, actually, Jake is a nurse at the clinic and he gave me the hookup. They're awesome. I'm telling you, if you get the vitamins, you'll lose weight faster than anybody else, and you'll win. It's a win-win. You look amazing and you win the prize money. Come on, do it."

"What's the name of the doctor?"

"He's at the Teeling's Clinic. Go to the BED group session and ask for Jake. I'll give you all the details. Trust me, you'll be happy with the results."

It sounded a little too good to be true. "And this is safe and legal?"

Karen shrugged. "Hey, no pain, no gain, right?"

A smile spread across my face. "No pain, no gain."

For the first time in a long while, I was hopeful. Maybe all I had needed was a few vitamins.

29

SELENA

Sprinting down the road, I made a sharp left and continued to run through the neighborhood filled with old homes and brown lawns. I didn't know where the feds had parked their van to listen in, but I had assumed it would be close by. Sure enough, the white van with a plumbing logo on the side of the door was parked in front of the second house. The door flew open, and I rushed toward it. After a quick glance inside, I climbed in. Mundy slid the door closed.

Sitting on the floor of the van, my chest heaved from the running and the fighting. I hadn't planned for Jake attacking me, but I got away, so that was all that mattered. He was a creep. Confirmed. I looked forward to Mundy and Deirdre slapping cuffs on him.

The driver started the van and high-tailed it out of the neighborhood. Nobody spoke until we were on the highway. "Are you okay?" Deirdre asked.

My breathing had steadied, and confidently, I said, "I'm fine. Trust me, I've dealt with worse than that guy."

"Well, we got some good footage. If that counts for anything."

I nodded. "It does. What do you make of the fact that Jake says he is pulling Teeling's strings, not the other way around?"

"We did a thorough background on..." Deirdre paused and exchanged a glance with Agent Mundy.

I helped them along and said, "I know his real name is Douglas Potter."

"Really? How?" Deirdre asked.

"I ran his plates and dug a little deeper."

Deirdre said, "Okay, well, we also looked into Potter, and he seemed to have some financial issues after they stripped him of his medical license. Maybe that's what they have on him. That and the fact that he's practicing medicine without a license."

I added, "If Potter isn't the person in charge, who is? I don't suspect Jake is the head of the operation. He doesn't seem quite smart enough, if you know what I mean."

Mundy said, "From what I've seen, I agree. We don't know who the head is, but we're sure there are others involved. The white house, where I met you the first time, is where they make the drugs."

Staring at Agent Mundy, I said, "That's what I suspected. The big barn garage would be perfect for cooking up some drugs."

Mundy nodded. "Exactly. We have surveillance pictures and have had a good look around. We're pretty sure that's the operation, and we're hoping to find out who the head is. I suspect Jake is small time - just following orders."

"How big is the drug operation? Do you think it's limited to the Bay Area, or are you thinking it's much bigger?" After learning what I had learned, I had my suspicions it was much bigger. They wouldn't send the FBI and DEA for one minor operation and one disgraced doctor - would they?

Agent Mundy said, "We think it's outside of California too."

"How extensive do you think the operation is?" I asked.

"We think they are operating out of at least three states — California, Oregon, and Nevada. So far, we haven't gotten close to the top, but we definitely know there's a top."

"You think the key is here in California?" I asked.

Deirdre said, "That's what I suspect."

"Why's that?"

"Because this is where the drugs are made, and we think they're distributing drugs from California to both Oregon and Nevada. We've been tracking Jake for a few weeks figuring he was doing the pill pick-ups, but this is the first time he's gone to the location where he picked up the drugs for you."

"Interesting. There are probably other stash houses in the Bay Area."

"That's what we think."

This was really a huge operation. Should I be less excited that I got to be a part of it? It was pretty cool. If I could help bring down a drug kingpin, that would be awesome. Despite my excitement, I tried to look stoic and not like a giddy newbie. Even though I was. "You think I did okay back there?"

Mundy said, "You did well. You were able to get some good information out of him. And you proved you can handle yourself back there. I just wished I could've seen the look on Jake's face when you fought back."

"It happened so fast - but I do recall seeing a bit of surprise in his beady little eyes."

"I bet." Deirdre chuckled.

"What now? I mean, should I go back to the clinic again after I kind of beat up Jake? Will it look weirder if I don't go back?"

Mundy said, "It's a good point. Maybe hold off on returning to the clinic for a day or two while we sort this out. Deirdre will go in to get a feel for the place and to monitor Jake to see if he comes back to work."

I said, "Sounds like the plan."

"We'll circle the parking lot for Jake's truck - if it's clear, we'll drop you back at your car."

I nodded in agreement with the plan. It was cool to feel like part of the team.

WE ENTERED THE PARKING LOT AT TEELING'S CLINIC. As planned, the driver drove up and down each aisle as the technician removed my wires. I kinda liked this undercover work and being wired up and working with the feds. Maybe a job in law enforcement wasn't completely out of the question after all? I could always be a PI for a few years and then go into to law enforcement. Well, considering I was three months shy of my twenty-second birthday, I had time to figure it out.

The parking lot was clear, and they dropped me in front of my car. After climbing out of the van, I glanced around the parking lot to make sure nobody was watching. There wasn't anybody around that I could see. I got into my car and drove back to my office. It had been a good day.

SEATED BEHIND MY DESK, I READ THROUGH MY FEW EMAILS and realized I should probably give Vicki an update. What could I say? That I was continuing to gather information? Yeah, that was what I would tell her until everything was resolved. I couldn't breech the FBI and DEA's confidentiality. Not to mention that would be a stupid thing to do. I picked up my phone and called Vicki.

She answered right away. "Hi, Selena."

"Hi, Vicki. How is Stephanie doing?"

"The doctor says she is stable. She has been going in and out of consciousness. She's pretty out of it with all the drugs that she is on. The doctor said he's hopeful. Knowing what drugs she was taking was critical so that they can assess her for future treatment and what signs to look out for in the future."

"That's good to hear."

"How's the case going? Any breakthroughs? Are the people who gave Stephanie the drugs any closer to being exposed?"

"I'm not sure about that. I'm still gathering information. Nothing concrete yet. I'll let you know when I have anything definitive and when we can bring it to the police." Lying to the clients - that was new.

"That's great. I appreciate all the work you've done. I'm sure Stephanie will be too as soon as she wakes up. When she is well enough for visitors, I'd love for you to come and talk to her. Is that something you could do?"

I said, "Of course." Part of me felt like I knew Stephanie from her diaries, but I had a feeling there was a lot more to her than her body issues.

"Thanks."

"Sure thing. Give my best to the rest of your family."

"Will do."

With my one client communication done for the day, I was ready to call it a night. Hmm. Maybe Dee would be up for tacos and margaritas. That could be good. I didn't drink often, but today had been an exciting day, and I kind of wanted to celebrate. With my mother and father's history of alcoholism, I usually stayed away from the stuff. But I had learned in all of my nine months of being twenty-one, and from my therapist, it was okay to have a sip now and then. I knew to stop if I was tempted to do more. Everything in moderation, right? Plus, Dee was hilarious when she had a few margaritas in her. Usually, she was a pretty serious person, but she definitely knew how to let her hair down and have some fun.

I felt like I could use some of that fun. Picking up my phone, I scrolled to my favorites and called Dee. No answer. Bummer. I left her a message, "Hey Dee. I wanted to know if you were up for dinner tonight. Maybe tacos? I'm heading home now. Call me."

Hopefully, she'd get back to me soon. Studying my outfit, I assessed I was a little worse for the wear. A wardrobe change was in order. A fresh outfit, some lip gloss, and a comb through my hair, and I'd be good to go. My computer powered down. I shut off the lights and headed out to the parking lot.

It was dark out with a sharp chill in the air. Wrapping my coat tighter around me, I hurried through the parking lot. The sound of squealing tires put me on guard. I turned to look where the maniac driver was coming from, but before I knew it, a dark van drove up, the door slid open, and a man in a mask grabbed me by the waist and put a hand over my mouth and threw me into a van. I kicked and bucked until I felt a sharp prick to my neck. My body relaxed, and the space turned dark.

30

SELENA

My head was pounding like it had been stuck in a vise. I lifted my head and studied my surroundings. The room was dark, and I didn't hear any noise aside from the wind outside. I didn't know why I had been taken to this location or who had brought me there, but I knew it wasn't good. It was bad. Terrible. Being tied to a chair in a dark room by unknown captors wasn't exactly my idea of a good time.

My last memories before waking up in this dark space replayed in my mind. A screech. A masked figure. Darkness. And now more darkness. Where was I? I wiggled my body to get a feel for the chair they had tied me to with a thick rope that was chafing my wrists and ankles.

The door creaked open, and someone flipped a switch, illuminating the room and burning my eyes. After adjusting to the light, a beefy man with a bald head and a gun on his hip stepped inside. Jake, sporting a black eye and scratches on his neck, followed behind.

The bald man said, "You're awake."

"Who are you? Why do you have me here?"

"I think the more pressing question is, what business do you have with my associate here?" Baldy asked.

Jake looked less than happy to see me. The scowl and hatred in his eyes weren't a good look.

"I don't know what you're talking about."

"Oh, really?" Baldy asked.

"Really," I said, rather sarcastically. Probably more sarcastic that I should've been for a person in my current situation. Looking around the space, I saw that it was small, about the size of my office. One window covered with a dark curtain. A small table and chairs in the corner. The main attraction - me - was in the center of the room.

"My associate here, Jake, told me that some little girl beat him up and stole my drugs."

Jake moved forward. "She didn't beat me up, but she stole the drugs."

Jake was moving slower than he had before. I had kicked him pretty hard with my boots. I wouldn't be surprised if he had bruised ribs, maybe even a crack or two.

Baldy continued, "Let's not mince words. You stole something that belongs to me. We brought you here because I don't tolerate that kind of thing around here, but when Jake told me how you got away so easily, I was interested in finding out more about you. Jake told me your name was Selena Jones, originally from LA. Imagine our surprise when we looked you up and followed you back to your office and found that you're not Selena Jones at all, but rather a Selena Bailey, private investigator."

Not good. "I don't like using my real name in therapy. I prefer to keep my professional and personal life separate." Was that believable?

"Is that right? Or are you undercover at the Teeling's Clinic?" Baldy asked, rather astutely.

"Why would I do that?"

"I don't know. That's why I asked. That's why you are here."

I didn't know how long this Q&A would go on for, but I didn't like it. I said, "You know, you could have just asked me. There was no need to abduct me and then hold me hostage."

"You make us sound so criminal," Baldy said, with a gleam in his eye.

"Okay, so I know who Jake is. Who are you? His boss?"

"I am."

"Well, then I'd rather talk to you than some low-level dealer like Jake."

Jake lunged at me, but the bald man put his arm out to stop him. "Calm down, Jake. She's just a little girl."

I rolled my eyes. He was one of those judge a book by its cover types.

"Ms. Bailey, I had my guys do some digging, and it turns out you're not only a private investigator but also kind of notorious for getting into stuff you shouldn't be getting into."

He wasn't *totally* wrong. "Was that a question?" I asked.

"It got me curious. Jake told me you were asking to see where the drugs are made. That you are some kind of drug dealer groupie. Looking at you, I'm guessing that's not true. Combine that with your chosen profession and your history of poking around in places that you shouldn't, I have the inclination to think that you're working for somebody. And I'd like to know who."

It didn't really take a genius to figure that out. Since I remained silent, he asked again, "Who are you working for?"

"You didn't answer my question. It's only fair if you want me to answer yours, you should answer mine. Who are you? What's your name?" I demanded.

Baldy pulled a chair from the corner and set it right in front of me and took a seat. He stared at me with his dark eyes. "I'm not sure you're in a position to make demands. But since you asked, just call me the boss. My given name isn't important. After all, I don't think we'll be in each other's company for long. Let's just get this over with, shall we? Who are you working for?"

"Like you said, I'm just a little girl who goes to a clinic to get skinny. I heard at Teeling's I could get some drugs to help me along. I just happen to also be a private investigator."

In a flash, his hands smacked me upside the head. My vision blurred, and my skin burned. I shut my eyes and reopened them to focus on the not-nice man sitting in front of me. He said, "Let's try that again. Who are you working for?"

I hadn't prepared for a back story if I were to be kidnapped and held hostage and then interrogated. I didn't want to give up Stephanie or any actual information, but I had to think quick for something believable. Relaxing my face to appear defeated, I said, "I'm working for myself. I got some intel that your operation was related to the human trafficking ring I came across in my past."

Baldy leaned back. "Who told you that?"

Of course, he would ask follow-up questions. "I have a source."

His eyes widened. "I'd say it's time to give up your source."

Who? Who, indeed. "A guy I met on the street. He said his name was Mikey. He ran drugs for the operation and said that they expanded to weight loss drugs and pointed me toward Teeling's. Mikey said you're all part of the same operation."

That made sense, right? If he knew I'd tussled with the traffickers before, it wasn't totally out of the question I'd still be after them.

Baldy folded his thick arms across his chest. "You know, Selena, you seem like a nice gal, but for some reason, I have the feeling you're not telling me the truth. I think you're working with someone, but you just don't want to tell me."

Okay, so he isn't a total dummy.

"Well, I'm not, and I don't appreciate being manhandled by your little errand boy over there."

Baldy said, "I'd be careful, Ms. Bailey. He's not as stupid as he looks."

Glancing over at Jake, I could see he obviously didn't appreciate the insult but didn't fight back. Baldy may be right. Jake was smart enough to sense there was something wrong with my story and had me followed almost immediately.

Based on my being tied up and the speed at which Jake alerted his organization, my only hope was to be rescued. I didn't have my car with the tracking device, but I did or should have my cell phone somewhere. They - the feds? Martina? - could put a trace out on my phone to find me. That was all assuming they were looking for me. I didn't have plans to meet up with anyone over the next few days, but I had called Dee and left a message. Assessing the room and the two men who stood in front of me, I hoped someone was looking for me. Otherwise, talking my way out was my only chance to get free. I said, "I have been looking for the traffickers for a few years now. I got a tip that maybe this was part of the group. Maybe my intel was wrong. Was it? Are you part of the trafficking organization that killed my boyfriend?"

It hadn't occurred to me that maybe they were part of the trafficking ring. Illegal drugs went hand-in-hand with that operation.

"That's a completely different ballgame. What we have here is very different, and what we have going on here is pretty damn good. I don't need some little girl coming in here trying to screw it all up because you want to play Nancy Drew."

"I take offense to that. I'm a real live person, not a character in a book. I'm a licensed private investigator." I paused to pull together a shred of confidence. "But, look, I hear you. You're not part of the trafficking ring, and you don't want me poking around. Fine. I'm done. Just let me go, and we'll act like this never happened."

"You know, you act pretty tough for someone tied to a chair." Baldy cocked his head. "You should be more cooperative. I'm still not convinced you're telling me the truth, but you know, I think we'll give you some more time to think about it. Maybe after a little rest, you'll be more cooperative."

What did that mean? Give me more drugs? But before I could contemplate the notion further, Jake came up behind me, wrapped his arm around my neck, and squeezed and squeezed until I lost consciousness.

"Hi there, sleepyhead."

Damn. I'm still here. My head pounded so hard I thought it would pop like an over-inflated balloon. I glared at the bald man and the two men with him. More goons? The additional muscle wasn't a good sign. Were they there to kill me and dismember my body? Would anyone ever find me?

"I hope you're more willing to talk now that you've had some rest. Now, I'll ask you one more time. Who are you working for?" I shook my head, and he said, "No. No. No. Selena, I need you to think very careful about the next words that will come out of your mouth." With that, he raised his enormous gun and pressed the nozzle to my temple.

It was basically my least favorite position to be in. I sat up straight and froze. I realized in that moment how badly my body shook, and nausea filled my belly. Not good. Did I have a concussion?

"Last time now. Who are you working for?" he asked before cocking the gun.

With tears streaming down my face, I said, "Okay, I'll tell you everything."

31

SELENA

BALDY LOWERED THE GUN AND STEPPED BACK TOWARD where Jake and the other icky man were standing. Baldy raised his dark brows. "Talk."

"Can I have a drink of water?" I asked, hoping to buy myself a little time. I wasn't naïve enough to think that even if I told them everything that they wouldn't still kill me, or worse. Oh, yes, I'd learned in my time there were things worse than death, and I had a feeling if they were gonna take me out, it wouldn't be a quick shot to the head. It might. I didn't really know for sure, but I didn't like the odds.

Baldy dipped his head toward Jake. "Go get her a bottle of water."

Maybe the bald man wasn't so terrible. As I quietly waited for Jake to return with my water, I mentally captured images of the men to commit to memory so that if I got out of this alive, I'd be able to describe them to a sketch artist.

How long had I been in the room? Where was I? Was I behind one of the stash houses? Were there neighbors who would hear me if I screamed out? And why hadn't anyone come looking for me? Maybe I hadn't been there that long? All I really knew at that point was that I didn't like being tied to a chair, I didn't like these drug dealers, and I needed to get out of there as fast as humanly possible.

Jake returned with the water.

At least I had tried to prolong whatever happened next. He walked up to me, unscrewed the cap, and pressed the bottle to my lips. I tilted my head back so that some of the water would go in my mouth and not just dribble down my chin and onto my shirt.

"Now talk," Jake commanded.

My voice shook. "Okay, this is the God's honest truth." I swallowed. "I was contacted a week and a half ago by a woman named Vicki Crawford. Her sister Stephanie had collapsed at her apartment. Vicki suspected her sister had been taking some kind of drug, or they gave something to her at Teeling's Clinic, which caused her to collapse. As part of the investigation, I went through Stephanie's apartment and found some pills in bottles labeled vitamins A and C, and they clearly weren't either, so I sent them to a lab to have them tested. I also did a little digging into the clinic and into the background of Dr. Teeling, also known as Douglas Potter, an unlicensed doctor from Florida. In the meantime, while the testing was going on, I went under-cover at the clinic as a patient to see if I could get the same drugs to verify they had come from the clinic. Vicki wanted me to expose the doctor to pay for what happened to Stephanie."

Hopefully he doesn't ask for more than that.

"What did you find?" Baldy asked.

"The lab said the drugs were Fen-Phen, fenfluramine and phentermine. One of them is illegal. So, I began to suspect that maybe there was an illegal drug operation for supplying the pills to the clinic, but when I finally got to meet with Dr. Teeling - Douglas Potter - he wouldn't give me any pills. I had seen Reba talking with Jake in a huddle, as if they were talking about something secret, so I took a chance and tried to get the pills from Jake. I think you know what happened after that. He took me to a house and then tried to sexually assault me. I kicked his ass and then ran."

Baldy began pacing. He said, "Interesting. You acquired a lot of information in a short amount of time."

"I am a private investigator."

"How were you planning to expose Teeling?" Baldy asked.

"Stephanie's sister wanted to make sure that the people who did this to her sister paid for what they did. I was trying to collect evidence, so I could bring it to the police."

"And have you brought the information to the police?" he asked.

"No, I haven't had the evidence until today. There was no exchange. And I don't have the evidence anymore since you took my backpack and my cell phone. I was actually looking forward to going out with a girlfriend for margaritas and tacos until you grabbed me. Look, I swear that is absolutely everything."

The bald man stopped pacing. He glanced over at the two other men behind me. "I tend to believe your story, but I have another concern."

Not good news for me. "What are your concerns?"

"You say this investigation is as innocent as a relative who suspected Dr. Teeling was practicing some shady medicine. How do I know you won't go to the police and tell them everything you know?"

"Well, first of all, I'll give you my word that I will not bring this to the police. I will tell Vicki I'm off the case. I have already given her the name of the drugs her sister was taking. I'll close out the case file."

"I wish I could believe you. From what we've learned, you

have single-handedly hunted human traffickers like a dog with a bone. Why would we think you'd just let us be?"

I mustered every bit of courage I had left and said to him, "They killed my boyfriend. And I couldn't let that go. I haven't let it go. I won't let it go." I wanted to kick myself as tears streamed down my face once again. "Vicki and Stephanie are just clients. They aren't my boyfriend, and they're not my family. They're just clients. I will let this go."

Baldy tapped his gun against his forehead. "You know Selena, I think I almost believe you. You seem smart and capable. You've kinda grown on me a bit, which is why this will be difficult."

My eyes widened. I never thought I'd plead for my life, but this was a situation where it was the only option, and I really didn't want to die. Through fresh tears, I said, "Please don't do this. I promise I'll let it go. If you've looked into my past, you'll know that if I'm gone, there are people who will hunt you down to find me. My stepmother is the best in the business. She's ex-Army and works with ex-special forces and they treat her and me like family. They will come after you."

Baldy cracked a smile. "Oh, yes, your stepmother, Martina Monroe. I learned a bit about her. She's not quite in the news as much as you are. But I saw she works at Drakos Monroe Security & Investigations. From what I hear, they're a pretty legit firm. What you say may be true, but she doesn't know what happened to you or where you are. There is nothing linking us to you. So, they can look, but they won't find us. Not only that, but they may think it was the traffickers who got a hold of you. Unfortunately, Selena, this is how we have to do things, and I'm sorry for that. Under different circumstances, I think maybe you and I could've been friends."

Doubtful. My wrists were already raw from the rope. There was no way to get out of them. If I could tip over the chair, I could try to wiggle out of the room. I didn't know how that would help, but at least I wouldn't be a sitting duck. I'd be a laying down duck. Was that better? I could head-butt somebody. But there were three of them. Escape was a fantasy.

Eyes shut, I said, "Fine, do what you have to, but there're notes on my computer. They're backed up on the cloud. They will find you."

That part was mostly true. All my notes were on my computer, and everything was backed up to the cloud, so even if they destroyed my computer, there was digital evidence of all the information I had on this case, minus the FBI and DEA part.

Staring into my eyes, Baldy asked, "Where do you keep your computer?"

"It's in my office, but since it's backed up to the cloud, it doesn't really matter. You kill me, I have no doubt the entire team at Drakos Monroe will come after you. If they can't find my body, chances are that, when your people coming looking for you, they won't find yours either."

When I planned the words, I was grandstanding, but when I said it aloud, I realized it was probably true. Martina wasn't one for vigilante justice, but I didn't think Stavros was above it.

We sat in silence as the boss contemplated what to do. "We need her to delete the information off the cloud. Jake, get her phone."

Dammit. Apparently, Baldy was a crime boss who knew that you could access everything from your phone - including the cloud. Although access to my phone wasn't necessarily a bad thing. I could call 9-1-1 for help. As Jake ran off, like the ever-ready errand boy he was, the boss leaned up against the wall. "You know, if I didn't have to kill you, I think I would try to hire you."

I shook my head in disbelief.

"You're pretty savvy."

"Thanks," I said, dryly.

"You know, I'd like to think if I ever had a daughter, she'd be like you."

"Really? Do you think she'd be tied up in a shed somewhere, about to be murdered by a bunch of drug dealers? That's what you envision?"

My full snark was coming out. These guys were going to kill me either way. I wouldn't delete the files. They'd kill me anyway, so why would I?

Jake returned with my phone and stepped toward me. "Password."

They would not let me type it in my phone, which meant calling for help was out of the question. I'd just have to act slowly to buy time until I could come up with a plan to get out of there alive - although I was all out of ideas. *It can't end this way. It just can't.* I said, "4-9-9-5"

He unlocked the phone and stared at the screen. Jake turned to the bald man. "She has a lot of missed calls. Someone could be looking for her. Maybe we should shut off the phone and worry about the files later. We have her password now. We could access it later, after we get rid of her, and then delete the files."

The bald man had been right. Jake wasn't as dumb as he looked. The boss said, "Good thinking. Get rid of her," before turning around to leave the shed.

Jake leaned down and put his lips to my ear. "I'm going to enjoy this."

32

STEPHANIE, AGE 25

M<small>Y</small> <small>EYELIDS FLICKERED OPEN</small>. I <small>LOOKED TO THE RIGHT AND</small> to the left. Mom, Dad, and Vicki were there. Did they ever go home? Nobody had explained to me why I was there. Although I wasn't sure that I'd been awake for more than a few minutes at a time. I was so tired, and it felt like there was someone sitting on my chest. Mom leapt from her chair. She must've just realized my eyes were open. I wished she would go home and get some rest. They didn't need to be there. "Mom."

"Oh, Stephanie, you're awake. I'm so happy. Can you hear me okay?"

She asked me that every time I opened my eyes. I nodded. "Yes." I turned my head, "Hi, Dad."

Dad, at my mom's side, said, "Hi, sweetheart. I'm glad you're awake."

I said, "Vicki."

She smiled widely. "Steph. How are you feeling?"

"I've been better," I mumbled.

They all laughed at that. They really needed to get some sleep. It wasn't that funny, but I was feeling stronger, despite all the tubes and lying in a hospital bed like a lump. "I am feeling a little stronger."

Vicki said, "That's great."

"Nobody's told me what happened. I don't know why I'm here. Do the doctors know why?" I asked.

My parents and sister exchanged glances. Almost like they didn't want to tell me, which was strange, considering it was my body. Vicki spoke. "Apparently, you have been taking some drugs from that clinic you were going to, and they caused damage to your heart valves."

They were supposed to be safe. He swore they were safe. That woman, what was her name? Dee-Dee? Deirdre? She had told me not to take them. I had told her I'd be fine. Reba said they were fine, and she'd been taking them for a while. "What were they?"

Vicki said, "Fenfluramine and phentermine."

"Are they that bad?" I asked.

Vicki explained, "They cause heart problems and lung problems too."

"How long have I been here?"

"It's been a few weeks."

"Oh." I knew I'd had surgery and that I'd collapsed. Did that mean I could have died from the diet pills? "How did you know I was taking diet pills?" The only people who knew I was taking the pills were the people at the clinic. I had been so happy I was losing so much weight.

Vicki looked over at Mom and Dad before she answered. "I hired a private investigator. She searched the apartment and found pills that didn't look right and had them tested. She's also been working undercover at the clinic to try to find out who was producing these pills. They are illegal. I wanted to make sure what happened to you didn't happen to anybody else."

"A private investigator? And she went through my things?"
My diaries. My personal things.

"Yes, I'm so sorry to invade your privacy. Selena, that's the private investigator, handled everything. I just wanted to know what was wrong. The doctors didn't know why you were having heart issues."

Maybe I had a problem. I hadn't ever considered that I actually had an eating disorder until I went to the group sessions at the clinic. I initially just went for the pills, but when I related to so many of the other people's stories, I had wondered if maybe I had a problem and that I needed real help. Of course, after I started taking the pills, I had brushed the thoughts aside, deciding that being thin was more important. My desire to be thin almost killed me. "You guys. I think I might have a problem."

Mom knitted her brows together. "Honey, what do you mean?"

"I think I might need to see a therapist. I think I might have an eating disorder."

My mother gasped as if shocked, yet there I was, lying in a hospital bed because I had taken diet drugs. Illegal diet drugs - just to be thin. "Honey, are you sure?" Mom asked.

I turned and looked over at Vicki.

She said, "Mom, I think Steph needs help. We should support her."

"Thank you, Vicki." I felt so weak. Not just physically but mentally, too. Finally acknowledging that I had a problem, since that problem had nearly cost me my life, I began to rethink a lot of things. Maybe all these years, it wasn't really my weight that I was struggling with because, from what I heard from those women in the group sessions, it was my emotions, my anxiety, and my depression I was struggling with. Eating was my solution to those problems and not the problem itself. I thought I was finally ready to get help, real help. I didn't want to live like that anymore. I wanted to be healthy and thrive - it was about time.

33

SELENA

Footsteps sounded toward the shed, causing all in the room to turn toward the doors. The bald man glanced back at Jake and the silent man who stood in the corner. "Are you expecting anyone?"

Jake shook his head. The silent man did the same.

My heart nearly pounded out of my chest. Someone yelled, "Selena, get down." Had I heard that right? I shook it off, and my instincts kicked in. I rocked and wobbled until my chair fell over onto the ground, and before I could call out, bullets flew through the shed. On my side, with the chair attached to me, I tried to inch toward the corner farthest away from the bald man.

In what seemed like a flash, the FBI had stormed the small space and Baldy, Jake, and the silent man were on the ground being cuffed. I glanced up, and my heart nearly stopped. I thought I was hallucinating. I eked out, "Martina."

She ran toward me, stepping over the men being cuffed on the ground. I heard the flick of a blade. She sawed off the ropes around my wrists and then went to work on the restraints binding my ankles. She lifted me off the ground. "Are you okay?"

"I guess. How did you find me?" How did she always find me?

Ignoring my question, Martina wrapped her arms around me as my body shook and my tears fell. Soon, we untangled, and a blanket was wrapped around me.

Peering across the room, I watched as the drug dealers were hoisted to their feet, and the officers marched them outside one by one.

Martina said, "Let's get out of here."

I nodded as she ushered me out of the shed and toward the front of the house that was surrounded by law enforcement vehicles.

When I finally calmed down and Martina and I were far away from the bad guys, I said, "I was so scared. Those guys were going to kill me. Like really kill me."

"They can't hurt you now."

"They told me some things."

"Like what?"

"Well, after I told them I was hired by Vicki and they were pleased with what I knew, they told me they couldn't let me go. I didn't tell them I was working with the FBI or the DEA. They didn't know that at all." I paused. The sound of sirens filled me with a sense of calm. I hadn't been killed. I hadn't thought they would find me in time. How had they found me? And what drug was I injected with? How long had I been knocked out? I continued, "I think they have more locations. They told me I couldn't ruin their operation. They have a big thing going, but also they aren't part of any kind of the trafficking rings which..."

Martina cocked her head. "What do you mean? Why would they tell you that?"

I explained how I had originally told the drug dealers I was working for myself so that they wouldn't go after Vicki or know about the FBI and DEA operation.

Martina said, "I suppose that's good."

Paramedics approached, and I wondered what I looked like. Probably a mess. My body ached. My head throbbed, and my wrists burned. Martina rubbed my arm. "Are you sure you're okay?"

"I'll be okay."

Behind the paramedics stood Deirdre and Mundy. "Selena, how are you hanging?" Mundy asked.

"I'll be all right. I didn't tell them I was working with you guys."

Deirdre said, "They know we're on to them now. I'm glad we got to you in time. We also have people searching the property and at the other home where we believe they are making the drugs. These guys are out of business."

"What about Teeling? I mean Potter. Will he get away with it?" I asked.

Mundy shook his head. "Nope. A team has already picked him up at his house."

Deirdre said, "Hopefully he talks. If he's smart, he will. We'll push him to reveal his blackmailers, which should help nail the coffin on these dealers. We think busting these guys will help us get the rest of them. This was a good start to taking down the entire operation. We owe that to you, Selena."

I didn't feel like I had accomplished much other than almost being sexually assaulted and killed. If I was feeling anything, it was stupid. Kidnapped and thrown in a van? It was a total cliché. I should have been more alert, more on my game. It had happened so fast. "Where are they now?"

Deirdre explained, "They're outside with an entire squad questioning them while the team searches the house."

Agent Mundy smirked. "Why, do you have a few words for them?"

I gave a coy smile, feeling some of my power returning. "You know, I may have a few words for them."

Deirdre said, "Well, now is your time to say whatever you'd like to them because, after we take them in, they'll be hard to get to. I could escort you over there if you'd like."

"I'd like that."

Deirdre turned to the paramedics. "Give us a few minutes."

"Yes, ma'am."

Martina squeezed my arm. "You know they will need to question you as well. This is a very serious situation, and it may take a lot out of you. You may want to save your energy."

"I'll be okay, Martina. I want to say my piece."

"Okay. I'll come too."

My three saviors led me over to where the prisoners were lined up.

Just minutes before, I'd felt like I was a crumpled piece of paper on the ground, about to be thrown away. My strength, at least my mental strength, was returning. They had almost taken me down - for good. What was the old adage? Almost doesn't count.

With the agents and Martina by my side, I strutted up to Baldy. "Oh, I don't think I mentioned that I'm also working with the FBI *and* the DEA," I said with a smirk.

Satisfaction filled my being as I stepped toward Jake and said, "And you're a creep, and you're lucky I didn't do more damage to your face," before turning to the left where the silent man stood.

I looked him up and down before saying, "I don't know you, but I'm pretty sure I don't like you either."

Finally, I refocused on the bald man - the boss. "I told you they would find you. You should've listened."

He shook his head. "None of this will stick."

"Are you kidding? They're raiding all your properties right

now. Not to mention they have you on kidnapping and attempted murder. That alone will put you away for life. You messed with the wrong girl, Baldy." With that, I turned around, deciding not to give them another ounce of my energy. At least not that day.

Facing Martina, I saw that she had a glimmer in her eye. I'd like to think it was pride. Deirdre said, "Well done, Selena. It's been good working with you. "

"'Thanks."

Mundy said, "We'll need official statements - but we can do that at the hospital. You've got a nasty bump on your head. You need to get it checked out."

"Okay. See you at the hospital, and..." I turned to Martina and then back to them. "Thank you for saving me."

Mundy nodded. "Any time."

I walked over to the paramedics. "Okay, I'm ready."

"We'd like to take you in the ambulance."

I turned to Martina. "You'll come to the hospital too, right?"

Martina said, "I'll ride with you in the ambulance."

"You don't have to do that. I'll be okay."

"I will ride with you. We can call your dad on the way to the hospital."

There was no arguing with Martina, and I was relieved. I didn't really want her to go - or to be alone. "Okay."

Martina had saved my life once again. If she were keeping score, I'd be working off my debts for the rest of my life.

34

SELENA

After what seemed like an eternity, the doctors finished poking and prodding me. Tests were run, and the results were in. *I'll live.* More specifically, I had a mild concussion with abrasions on my wrists and ankles. Not too bad, considering what the alternative could have been. I was beyond thankful that Martina and the rest of the team had arrived when they did. If they hadn't, I would've struggled and fought, but the reality was I had maybe three minutes before my life would have been over.

In the past, I had gotten myself into some tricky situations. It hadn't even been the first or second time I had a gun put to my head, but this experience was the very first time I'd actually thought I was going to die. Alone. In a storage shed.

The nurse pressed a few buttons on my IV pole and said, "All right, hon, I'll let your visitors know they can come in now. You take care, hon."

"Thanks." As much as I hated being in a hospital bed, it was better than being tied to a chair in the company of a bunch of creeps.

Footsteps sounded.

I called out, "Dad."

He rushed over and squeezed my hand. I winced.

"I'm so sorry. Is that okay?" he asked.

"It's fine. I'm just a little sensitive." My fingers weren't damaged - just the wrists, which were bandaged up pretty good, but any pressure was a little uncomfortable.

He said, "I'm so glad you're okay."

"Me too," Martina added.

Dad's brown eyes filled with tears.

I assured him, "I'm okay."

"You know, when I had a daughter, I didn't know just how often I'd be worrying about her. I think you never know until you have one. Not only do I have a daughter with a dangerous job to worry about but also a wife with a very dangerous job." Dad wiped his eyes with the backs of his hands. "I suppose I have a penchant for tough women."

Dad wrapped his arm around Martina.

"I'm so glad to see you both, but Martina, I never had time to ask - how did you find me? Where was I, and how long was I gone? Honestly, it's all a blur. They picked me up at my office and threw me in a van. It all happened so fast. I don't even know what day it is."

Martina nodded. "You can thank Dee for us finding you. She called me and said that you left a message to get together for dinner, but then when she called you back and you didn't respond or answer any of her texts or voicemails, something in her gut didn't feel right. So, I went by your office and saw your car in the parking lot, but you were nowhere to be found, and you didn't answer my phone calls or texts either. That's when I contacted agents Mundy and Long. We've been looking for you ever since. We finally got a tail on Jake. The team followed him, and he led us to where they were keeping you. Once we were pretty sure you were there, we put the team in place, and as soon as we had the green light, we went in and got you."

My debts to Dee, Martina, and Dad were piling up. There was nothing I wouldn't do for them. All three had saved my life - at least once. What would I do if I didn't have them? The honest answer was, I didn't think I would be doing much. I would be six feet under.

"I think I owe Dee that dinner. My treat."

"I think she'd like that. I called her while we were waiting for the doctors to finish up to let her know you're okay. She'd probably like a call from you, though."

"Thanks. I'll call her later. What day is it?" I asked.

Martina said, "It's Friday night."

"They had me for two days?"

Martina said, "Yes."

"Is Zoey still coming home tomorrow?"

Martina said, "She is, and she's excited to see you. We were all so worried, Selena."

I could only imagine. "I'm not gonna lie." I stopped as my voice started cracking. "I didn't think I was going to make it. I didn't think you'd find me in time. But I told them that I knew if they did something to me, you would come after them. I told them that."

Martina tilted her head. "It kills me that this happened to you. I wish you weren't working alone."

"Technically, I wasn't. I was working with the FBI and the DEA but..."

Martina added, "That was just for one part of the job. This job is dangerous, and if anybody can do it, you can, but you seem to have this knack for finding yourself in some really, really dangerous situations."

I shrugged. "I guess I'm just lucky that way."

Heavy footsteps approached, and I waved to Mundy and Deirdre. "Hey, thanks again for saving my life."

Agent Mundy said, "Any time."

"How are things going with the case? Did you put them in jail forever? Did you get the whole operation?" I knew it had probably only been a few hours, but I could hope.

Mundy chuckled. "Things don't happen quite that fast. But we have arrested an additional twelve people who were part of the drug organization and Douglas Potter a.k.a. Dr. Teeling."

Deirdre added, "One of those twelve was Reba from the clinic. Apparently, she was acting as a scout for Jake. She basically checked out the new members to make sure they wouldn't tell anyone about the drugs. It explains why I couldn't get access to the drugs. I hadn't passed her test."

That's wild.

Mundy added, "There are also things in motion to shut down the clinic."

I said, "Oh, no."

"Oh, no, what?" Deirdre asked.

I glanced over at Deirdre. "I think those people really need help. Where will they go for therapy? Those people are really hurting. Will they be notified the drugs are dangerous?"

Deirdre said, "Yes, all the patients will be notified, and they'll be referred to a new center for therapy."

"Good. Do you think you have enough evidence to prosecute? I know you said it doesn't happen right away, but does it, at least, look promising?"

Mundy and Deirdre exchanged glances. Mundy said, "We'll definitely build a case again Jake Barberry, Joe Terrence - that was the man you referred to as Baldy, and then the other guy was Joe Terrence Jr. - Baldy's son. The fact that they were holding you hostage and were clearly planning to end your life means all three will almost certainly go away for life. We did everything by the book to ensure there were no procedural mistakes to get them off. As far as the drug operation, we'll likely be able to tie them to that, but it will take some time while we wait for the forensics, witness statements, and the whole nine yards to make sure we have a solid case for the drug operation. I know it ended in a pretty sticky situation for you, but you did really great work. You're a valuable asset. If you ever consider joining the bureau..."

Deirdre said, "Or the DEA."

Mundy added, "You call me, and I'll pull a few strings to get you inside."

After working with them for the last week, it made me realize maybe law enforcement would be an interesting career path to take.

Being a private investigator meant that I could solve crimes that law enforcement couldn't or wouldn't, but helping take down a dangerous organization as part of the FBI was pretty cool. I supposed I'd have a lot to think about while I healed and was on break from work. "Thanks, I'll let you know."

Mundy looked over at Martina and Dad and then me. "We would like to take your full statement now. Your parents are welcome to stay if you want, or we can talk to you alone."

Before I could respond, Dad said, "Selena, if you don't mind, I kinda don't want you out of my eyesight for a little while. Is that okay?"

I nodded.

Mundy said, "Understood, but know that it may be a little difficult to hear."

Dad said, "It's okay. I don't want to leave her." He squeezed my shoulder.

I said, "Okay, let's get this over with."

"You got it." Mundy and Deirdre grabbed some chairs and turned on the tape recorder, and I told them everything that had happened from the moment I stepped out of my office until they came rushing in to save me. I wondered if I was a cat in a former life. They say cats have nine lives. If that were true, I thought I only had a few left. The question was, what would I do with them?

35

SELENA

Out of bed for the first time that day, I carefully slid my jeans on underneath my hospital gown. I was getting out. Thank goodness. After I chucked off the hospital gown, I slipped on a T-shirt and then a black hoody over it. Martina had gone to my house, rather the room I rented in a house, to get me some fresh clothes. When Martina had returned with my things, we'd discussed the idea of me moving in with them for a while. I was tough, and I was strong, but I couldn't hide the fact that the experience changed me. I didn't want to be scared, and I didn't want to hide, but I knew I needed to heal for a little while. Martina said she already had the room made up for me. She always did. They had a four-bedroom house, and there were two rooms always made up, one for me and one for Zoey when she came to visit. I hated the idea of losing my independence, but I liked the idea of having the comfort of family while my concussion and my pride healed.

Fully dressed, I walked out to the hallway of the hospital. Dad and Martina, as well as Mundy and Deirdre, were waiting for me. "Okay, well, I suppose it's convenient that I'm in the hospital. It saves us a trip," I said, attempting to make light of the situation.

Stephanie and I were in the same hospital, and since Mundy and Deirdre needed to speak with her about the investigation, we figured all three of us would go together. I didn't have my phone and couldn't call Vicki or Stephanie myself, but based on the information we had, the FBI looked up Vicki Crawford's phone number. They made the call and said that I would come by with them.

Since I already had a relationship with Vicki, it made sense I would go in first. I'd never met Stephanie, and I was looking forward to it. But that wasn't the only purpose of my visit. We hoped Stephanie could help us by connecting some dots between Teeling's Clinic and the drug operation.

We took the elevator up to the fourth floor, exited, and then headed toward Stephanie Crawford's room. The group stopped at the nurse's station to wait until I confirmed Stephanie was up for additional questioning. Standing in front of her room, I confirmed her name on the wall plate. *Check.* If what Agent Mundy and Deirdre had said was true and I helped bring down the dangerous drug operation, then it was because of Stephanie. It was because of Stephanie that I had investigated the clinic and crossed paths with the FBI and the DEA. Stephanie may have saved many lives. I knocked lightly on the door that was slightly ajar. The doorway widened, and Vicki Crawford stood before me, her eyes wide as she studied my appearance. "What happened to you?"

"It's kind of a long story. I'll tell you, but I was thinking maybe Stephanie might want to hear about it too."

"Absolutely. Please come on in. My parents are here too."

"Great." I followed Vicki toward the bed nearest the window. A middle-aged couple sitting in plastic chairs on one side of the bed, I presumed, were Stephanie's parents.

Stephanie was in the hospital bed propped up, which I understood was a good sign. I waved silently.

Vicki said, "Mom, Dad, and Steph, this is Selena Bailey, the private investigator I told you about."

Stephanie said, "It's nice to meet you. What happened to you?"

"Well... I'm not sure if you want all the gory details?"

"Did this happen while you were investigating the clinic?" Vicki asked.

"Yes. I have an update, actually."

Stephanie said, "I'd like to hear everything, if that's okay?"

I nodded and told them everything about the investigation from start to finish and to the current status. Mrs. Crawford, Stephanie and Vicki's mother, gasped. "Our daughter was going to a clinic that was connected to an illegal drug operation, and that drug operation kidnaps and murders people?"

"Apparently so. But the good news is Agent Mundy and Agent Deirdre Long are convinced they will be able to fully prosecute the ringleaders. Hopefully, they won't be able to distribute illegal drugs anymore. What happened to Stephanie shouldn't happen to any other people."

Vicki shook her head. "I'm so sorry we did this to you, Selena. It's because I hired you that you were almost killed."

"It's not your fault. Trust me, this isn't my first hostage situation," I said with a shrug. "I tend to attract danger or look for it, depending on who you ask. I'm glad you hired me, Stephanie and Vicki, because if you hadn't, the FBI said they weren't sure they could crack the case or how much longer it would take them. Because we teamed up, we could resolve the case much quicker. That means fewer people will take the illegal drugs and develop dangerous conditions or worse - there were others who didn't make it."

Stephanie said, "All of this because of the pills I got from Jake?"

"Yes. And for the record, Jake is not my favorite person."

"He's kinda gross," Stephanie commented.

"You have no idea. But don't worry, I gave him a black eye and a few cracked ribs."

A small smile formed on her lips, and I thought Stephanie seemed to enjoy that.

Vicki said, "Thank you, Selena. It sounds like you're incredible at what you do. If there is anything we can ever do to repay you, please let us know."

I glanced around the room and back at Stephanie. "Actually, there is. Agent Mundy and Agent Long are downstairs. They would like to take a statement from you about your time at the clinic. Specifically, how you got the drugs. They also want you to testify when you're strong enough. It'll really help the case against the drug operation."

I held my breath, hoping she would do the right thing. Not everyone could handle being a witness in such a big case. And I understood why. She could get threats against her and her family. It wasn't a decision to take lightly.

Stephanie said, "I'll do it."

"That's good to hear. Trust me, it's not easy to be involved in these cases. I may look young, but I've been in this game for a while."

Vicki said, "Dee said you were the best."

"Dee," I said with a chuckle. "Dee is the one who's the best. It's because of her they could find me when they did. We were supposed to go out for tacos and margaritas, but when she called me to make plans, she couldn't get a hold of me. She put two and two together and called my stepmother, and now here I am."

Vicki added, "Dee said you two had worked some investigations together."

"Yeah, Dee actually worked with me for a short time at my stepmother's security and investigations firm. She decided it wasn't for her."

Vicki said, "Well, I think she has a very bright future as a psychiatrist."

"I think so too."

That reminded me I owed Dee tacos and margaritas - for life.

"All right, well, I'm going to let the agents know you're ready to make a statement. Are you ready, Stephanie?"

Her mom stepped up closer to Stephanie and took her hand. "Honey, if you're not strong enough right now, we can have them come back later."

Stephanie shook her head back and forth. "No, I'm up for it. After everything I've just heard, I want to make sure these people go to jail forever. I don't want somebody else to be lying in a hospital bed because they took some diet pills."

Her mother looked up at me. "Okay, you can tell them to come in now."

"It was nice meeting all of you, and, Stephanie, you take care."

"Thanks, Selena. It looks like you could use some rest yourself."

I shrugged. "That's what the doctors are saying." I waved and exited the room, heading toward the nurses' station to let the agents know Stephanie was ready to make a statement.

Once I notified them, I entered the elevator and made my way down to the lobby to meet Dad and Martina. As the elevator descended, I felt lighter. With Stephanie's witness testimony and maybe others from the clinic, I was confident those responsible for the deaths of the two other women, Kelly and Alex, at the clinic and Stephanie's heart valve issues, would be held accountable for what they did. They had kidnapped and decided to kill me at the drop of a hat, so who knows what else they had done. I just hoped the trial was swift, so we could put this behind us sooner rather than later.

36

SELENA

SITTING ON THE BED IN MY OLD BEDROOM IN MARTINA AND Dad's house, I reflected on the last four years. There were so many ups and so many downs, it seemed a little crazy to find myself back in that room again.

When I had first met Martina and reconnected with my dad, I had also just been kidnapped, almost murdered, and they took me in right away - after saving me. It was practically déjà vu, except I was four years older. I'd like to think I was wiser, yet the outcome was the same. Luck had been on my side once again.

Suddenly, the room felt larger, or I felt smaller. I couldn't tell which. My therapist would surely tell me I was bigger and stronger than before. This was just a momentary setback, and I just needed a little time to heal and get back to one hundred percent. Not that I doubted that was true, but it didn't make me feel any better in that moment. My therapist would probably also tell me to feel my feelings and that it was perfectly okay and healthy to be feeling down. My body would heal, and so would my mind.

Having heard it all before, something about this latest event felt different. Maybe it was because I was older, and knew I had a lot to lose, that this new loss of peace and safety hit me harder. When I was seventeen, I wanted to live, but I did not know how good life could actually be - now I did.

When I chose an interesting and dangerous job, I hadn't considered the times when it would be lonely or, if I was doing mostly background checks - boring. Never would I have thought after only a few weeks, I would have run back to Martina and Dad's safe, loving home. Maybe I wasn't as grown-up as I thought. Maybe I wasn't ready to face the world all by myself, and maybe the greatest thing about that was I didn't have to. I got knocked down, but I had my family to help pick me back up again. That was the most miraculous thing of all, really.

That wasn't the only epiphany I had. The other was that when I had healed enough, my butt was getting back to the shooting range so I'd be ready to apply for my conceal and carry license. A gun was far more effective than a baton in a situation where it was my life or theirs. I wouldn't make that mistake again.

A knock on my door drew my attention to the clock sitting on my nightstand. It was almost time for dinner. "Selena, are you in there? Are you decent?"

The sound of Zoey's voice always lightened me. "I'm dressed, but I can't claim to be decent. You can come in," I said with a chuckle.

The door creaked open, and there stood Zoey, wide-eyed, with her dark hair flowing practically to her waist. I stood up and wrapped my arms around her. She whispered in my ear. "I'm so glad you're here and that you're safe."

"Me too."

She stepped back and quietly shut my bedroom door before saying, "Mom told me everything. It must have been so terrifying."

"I admit, it wasn't fun."

"You are one tough sister. I swear between you and my mom, I don't know two tougher women."

"I try. Maybe one day, I'll be a Martina."

"I think you're pretty close to being there."

I didn't know about that. "Enough about me. How are you?" I was tired of talking about my ordeal and wanted to take a break from it all, at least for the night.

"I'm fantastic." Zoey told me about the new research opportunity she was taking part in at UC Davis Veterinary School. Zoey had always loved animals, and after starting out as a computer science major in college, she'd later switched to biology to prepare her to attend veterinary school. When she'd received acceptance to the Oregon State University's School of Veterinary Medicine, she'd been the happiest I had ever seen her. She said in a low voice, "And guess what? I haven't told Mom yet but..." She lifted her hand and showed me a ring on her left finger. "I'm engaged."

I stared at the sparkling stone on her hand. Engaged? To who? I tilted my head toward her. "Umm... more details, please."

"I know, I know. Mom hasn't met him yet, and nobody from the family has, but I met someone - he's great- and he just proposed!"

What? I swore my hearing must be impaired. "Who is this guy? How did you meet?" I was more than a little concerned over the seemingly fast-paced romance.

"He goes to school with me, but he's about to graduate. We've been dating for the last couple of months. I haven't said anything because I wanted to bring him home to meet Mom and Charlie and you, of course. My other friends think he's great."

Mind blown. "When did he propose?" I was completely shocked by this news. It wasn't like Zoey to hide a boyfriend, and now she was engaged? I didn't think Martina would like this one bit.

"Well, so, he's actually in the car right now. He came with me on the research trip, and he proposed earlier today. I want to tell Mom, but I want her to meet him first. I'm telling you because I need your advice." She brought me over to my bed, and we sat down facing one another. "Mom's a little overprotective. How do I tell her?"

Of all the sticky situations I'd been in, I didn't envy Zoey's. "I don't know. This is crazy. No, it's not crazy. It's surprising. I'm so happy for you, Zoey. If this is the man you love and you want to get married, I'm so happy for you."

"He is the love of my life. He's the one," she declared.

"Congratulations. I can't wait to meet him."

"I can't wait for you to meet him, too. Back to the Mom situation, how do I tell her? Should I ease her in or rip off the Band-Aid?"

I contemplated Zoey's predicament. I wondered how she'd gotten past Martina with the ring on her finger. Martina wasn't one who didn't notice things - she noticed everything. "Are you sure your mom didn't already see the ring?"

"It was in my pocket. I just put it on," she said, with teeth gritted and a sparkle in her eyes.

For the first time in days, I laughed so hard my belly ached. "Girl, I do not envy you."

"It's bad, right?"

I nodded, and then Zoey joined me in a fit of giggles.

A knock on the door silenced us. "Yes?" I asked.

"Everything okay in there?" Martina asked through the door.

I turned to Zoey. "You have to tell her - like now. Before she meets him."

Zoey got up and opened the door.

Martina stepped in with a puzzled look. "What are you two laughing about?"

I opened my mouth to speak, but then stared at Zoey and said, "Zoey has something to tell you."

Zoey's bright blue eyes widened wider than I'd ever seen before. I glanced back at Martina, who looked a little stricken. "Zoey, what is it?"

Zoey looked petrified. I said to her, "It'll be okay."

"Well, Mom, there's something - there is someone I want you to meet."

Martina remained frozen in place. "Oh, you have a friend?"

Zoey eyed me. "He's my boyfriend, and we're very serious, and we're very much in love. He's actually here."

I watched Martina's expression change from fear to apprehension. "Your boyfriend is here?"

Zoey was practically dancing around, trying to suppress her energy. I could tell she wanted to tell Martina so badly but was also terrified of how she may react. "He's in the car. And we're engaged." She lifted her hand to show Martina the diamond ring on her finger.

Martina's mouth dropped open, and her eyes were wide. "You're what?" The look in Martina's eyes washed away our earlier giddiness.

Zoey explained, "We're engaged. He is a student, and he just proposed. It's been a whirlwind. I want you to meet him. He's waiting in the car." She said it as if trying to convince her mother that she wasn't making a big mistake.

She hadn't asked, so I didn't offer my opinion, but I thought she was too young, and it seemed a bit rushed. The family hadn't even met him. Martina would surely do a full background check, including criminal and employment - you name it. I wouldn't be surprised if she put a surveillance team on the guy.

Martina stood still - too still. She said, "Why don't you have him come in the house, so we can meet him?" and walked out of the room without another word.

I glanced back up at Zoey. She said, "Well, that went better than I thought, right?"

"I mean, yeah?" I shrugged. "You're going to get married. You're going to the chapel, and you're going to be married..." I sang to her.

She smiled again. "Mom will come around, right? I can't wait for you to meet him."

"I look forward to it."

After Zoey ran out of the room, I shook my head and thought, *Oh, Zoey.* That was something I was not expecting. I remained in my room until I heard the front door open and close, along with the sound of four footsteps and Martina and Dad's voices.

Hurrying to the hallway, I approached with a grin.

After handshakes, Zoey turned to me and said, "And, Henry, this is my sister, Selena."

I shook his hand. "Nice to meet you, Henry."

"You too. I've heard a lot about you, and I'm glad to hear you're safe."

"Thanks."

Martina looked at me and then looked at Zoey after doing a full once over of Henry. Martina said, "Why don't you all settle into the dining room? I'll bring in the appetizers."

Dad headed back to the kitchen, but Martina hurried over to me as Zoey and Henry made their trek to the dining room. Martina said, "Don't worry. I'm going to learn everything about Henry."

"Full background?" I asked.

"You better believe it. You want in on this?"

I smiled widely. "Absolutely."

Zoey's happiness meant the world to us. Both Martina and I knew enough of the dangers of bad relationships, and we would make sure that Zoey wasn't entering one. We would learn everything about Henry. Where he was born, where he grew up, his employment records, criminal history, his aspirations, and his character. It was far better to be safe than sorry. "Excellent. Now let's go get to know this guy," Martina said with a smirk.

As surprising as Zoey's engagement was, the news made sure that I wasn't the center of attention. And I'd much rather plot with Martina to find out more about Zoey's fiancé than discuss my latest ordeal further.

Over dinner, we caught up with Zoey and learned everything about Henry. Zoey protested only a few times about us interrogating him. But he seemed to be a good sport, which was a good sign. We would certainly verify all the information he gave us, so if he was smart, he would be prepared. I helped Martina clear the dishes from the table, despite protests that I had just been released from the hospital. *I can carry a few plates.*

After setting the dishes down next to the sink, I turned to find Martina was right behind me. She turned to me. "How are you feeling?"

I nodded. "I'm okay. Better."

"That's good. I'm really proud of you. You've overcome so much in your short life, and with each new setback, you come back stronger than ever. I really admire that. I have no doubt that this latest experience will only make you stronger, too."

"Thank you, Martina."

She set down the dishes. "And while I have you here - away from Zoey and her fiancé." She shook her head at the idea. "I wanted to talk to you earlier, but then Henry happened. Well, I wanted to tell you I've been thinking about you, your career, and I know I've told you before that you always have a job at Drakos

Monroe if you want it - but I have a serious proposal for you. I know you have a lease on your office for Bailey Investigations, but if you'd like to come back to Drakos Monroe on a trial basis, you could work in your office before deciding to commit and then if you do decide to join Drakos Monroe permanently you can sublet the office and maybe use that money for a down payment on an apartment - when you're ready. And if you decide not to come back, you keep the office and Bailey Investigations - no problem."

"Oh." That was all I could say to that. Did she really think I couldn't make it on my own, or did she just really want me back at Drakos Monroe? I had to admit working on my own had been, well, lonely and dangerous and kind of scary.

Martina continued, "And if you decide you want to stay at Drakos Monroe, you will come in as a staff member. I love and admire your independent spirit, but I think you can probably now understand the benefit of having a team behind you. I will always be there to support you, whether you're with Drakos Monroe or remain independent with Bailey Investigations. But I've already talked to Stavros about bringing you back full time. You can have some time to think about it, but we have an opening, and we'd like you back."

Martina had always said I could come back to Drakos Monroe if my independent gig didn't work out, but the fact she had already spoken to Stavros meant she was serious. Part of me thought if I went back now, I'd be giving up - throwing in the towel. It wasn't my style. However, I hadn't realized how lonely the job would be or how much I missed working with other people and having a team. "I appreciate the offer, Martina. Can I have a little time to think about it?"

"Of course."

"Okay, I'll think about it."

"And you know you can stay here as long as you want. I just

mentioned you getting an apartment because maybe when you're ready, you would like to have an apartment instead of renting a room out of someone's house. Maybe you could have your own kitchen, and you can have your own bedroom and bathroom and living room area, and you could have friends over."

"I think I'd like that too." I did. I really did. After seeing Stephanie's grown-up apartment, I had been envious. If I signed on with Drakos Monroe, I'd be able to afford it with the steady paycheck.

"Okay, well, I wanted to let you know that I've been thinking of you, and the offer stands, but if you could please let us know within a few weeks because otherwise, we will hire another private investigator for the team. We have more work than we know what to do with."

"Okay, I promise I'll think about it and let you know."

She gave my shoulder a squeeze before heading back into the dining room. I had a lot to think about. How important was it for me to have my own private investigations firm? To be independent and make all my own decisions and not have to follow anybody else's rules, except the law? What was the right path for me? So far, within a few weeks, I had already almost been killed. If I hadn't been working with the feds, I would probably be swimming with the fishes. And that didn't seem very appealing. Martina's offer was a good one. I would have to get some rest and think about it. I wasn't sure I was ready to give up on Bailey Investigations just yet.

37

SELENA, 6 MONTHS LATER

After plating the fish tacos, rice, and salad, I carried them over to my new dining table where Dee sat waiting for her dinner. I set one plate in front of her and one at my place setting. Seated, I said, "I present to you fish tacos a la Selena."

Dee smiled. "I am very impressed, Ms. Bailey."

The taco dinner was a thank you to Dee for saving my life, for being my best friend, and for basically always being there for me when I needed her. There was so much that had happened since the day Dee and I met.

At the time, I hadn't realized how much Dee would change my life. It was amazing how two people could come together randomly yet have such profound impacts on each other's lives. Dee was my roommate my first year in college. We had never met before. I thought we wouldn't be friends, but she had been kind to me - a dark, quiet, strange girl who kept to herself. She brought me out of my shell and encouraged me to enjoy college life and life in general.

We had worked together; we had laughed together; we had lived together, and we had cried together. And now we were both embarking on new journeys again. "I'm so glad you could make it tonight. You've been such a busy bee lately. It was hard to get you here."

Dee said, "I know it's been super crazy with all these interviews for medical school, but I have some news. I am very excited to tell you..."

Smiling, I asked, "Did you choose which school you're going to?" Ms. smarty-pants Dee had been accepted into multiple medical schools. I wasn't surprised. Dee was the smartest person I knew and had a passion for helping others in a way that I hadn't seen in anyone else. She was determined to be a psychiatrist and help those who had suffered trauma. She wanted to make their lives better and let them see they could turn around their trauma and be stronger because of it. Dee said she wanted to be a part of that process. "I decided... drumroll please."

I stared at her, eager with anticipation.

"Stanford. I'm going to Stanford Medical School." Dee squealed in delight.

"Congratulations." I got up, ran around the table, gave her a hug, and said, "I'm so proud of you, Dee."

"Thank you."

My excitement was a little selfish. Don't get me wrong, I was excited for Dee that she had been accepted into one of the top medical schools in the country but also that she wasn't leaving the Bay Area. I wasn't going to lose her to Johns Hopkins, all the way across the country, or to some other state where I would hardly get to see her. Although she told me that medical school would be demanding and her time would be limited, the fact that she would be just across the bridge meant that I could see her far more frequently than if she'd gone out of state. We both wiped away our tears of joy. I sat back down. "It's so cool."

"Isn't it?" Dee asked in astonishment.

"It is. I must admit, I'm super happy that you're staying in the Bay Area."

"I'm happy I'm staying here too. My future is set for the next four years. How are you settling into your new normal?" Dee asked with a bit of playfulness.

It had been six months since I'd started back up at Drakos Monroe Security & Investigations. I had done what Martina had suggested, which was to come back on a trial basis and keep my Bailey Investigations office. That situation had only lasted a month. I was so happy to be back using the most state-of-the-art equipment and to get to work alongside a team of top tier professionals; it was like coming home. It was home.

Drakos Monroe Security & Investigations were a family, and as much as I liked the idea of having my name on the building, the extra security and support, and a steady paycheck were nice. More than nice.

After subletting my office to a person starting up their own insurance company, I used that money, like Martina had suggested, and rented my very own apartment. My physical scars from the kidnapping had healed, and I thought my mind had too. Martina wasn't wrong. I felt stronger than I was before.

And maybe the lesson had been knowing when it was better to *not* go it alone. It wasn't defeat; it was being smart. "I love it."

"You don't miss your old gig?"

"Well, I only had the old gig for less than a month. And the pay wasn't very good, and I almost died. It's nice to have a paycheck and my own apartment. Plus, I get to see Martina every day. That's nice."

Dee nodded. "I think it suits you."

"I think so too. I think it was important that I went on my own and tried it, even if just for a little while. Now I don't ever have to wonder what it would have been like because I know. I think you're right. I think Drakos Monroe is exactly where I should be. I mean, I can't tell the future, but for now, there's no better place for me to learn and grow as a private investigator. Plus all the cool toys!"

Dee laughed. "I know how you like bugging places and setting up security cameras."

"True, true." I couldn't afford any of that equipment on my own. With the resources and experience at Drakos Monroe, it was definitely the right decision and the right place for me to be. "I bet your boyfriend's pretty happy that you're staying in the Bay Area too."

"He is."

The way Dee said it made me think there was something behind it. Oh, God, was she engaged like Zoey? Henry's background came back clean, but both Henry and Zoey agreed they would slow down a bit and have a long engagement - much to Martina's relief.

Dee said, "We are moving in together."

"Congratulations." Thank goodness she wasn't getting married. She was only twenty-two! Twenty-two was too young, right?

Dee was grinning from ear to ear. "Yeah, we're both pretty smitten with each other and with my crazy schedule and his crazy schedule, we figured this way, we'll be able to see each other more."

"That's great. I'm thrilled for you."

"Me too."

I said, "We've come a long way, kid."

Dee started laughing. "You know I'm actually older than you, right?"

Dee and I continued to eat tacos and chat about how far we had come in the last four years. We were both happy and excited about our futures. Not something we would've said a few years ago.

These last six months, I had learned that it is okay to make mistakes, to try different things, and to go with your heart, your gut, and what feels right. Perfection is a myth and flawlessness is an illusion. The most any of us can do is continue to learn, grow, and be the best version of ourselves we can be.

THE END

A NOTE FROM H.K. CHRISTIE

Dear readers,

I hope you enjoyed *Flawless*. Like the other books in the Selena Bailey series, I did extensive research on the topic covered (throughout my adult life as well as specifically for this book). There is so much I could have included about diet culture, why 'diets' don't work, body positivity, body neutrality, eating disorders, the patriarchy and the expectations bestowed upon on men and women that have caused so much harm to our society (and you really don't want to get me started about Fen-Phen and how it's too similar to what is currently going on with the Opioid crisis) - I didn't because then it would have been more of a text book and actually a pretty complex one at that. But, I am going to give you a quick definition of diet culture because it is easily misinterpreted.

Diet culture is defined as, "**a rigid set of expectations about valuing thinness and attractiveness over physical health and emotional well-being**" (from www.choosingtherapy.com).

My top personal takeaways after researching and writing

this book (and I encourage you to do your own research or seek professional advice since I'm not a medical doctor or psychologist) has been this: diets don't work and are a recipe for weight gain in the long run, eating disorders are *very* complex, weight alone doesn't determine whether you are healthy (ie a bigger person can be healthier than a smaller person), mental health is as important as physical health (and really I think they're are highly correlated), food is often the solution not the problem (think back to Stephanie's sadness over a break up - the sadness was fixed with food leading her to a lifetime of emotional eating), *words matter* at all ages (think back to Stephanie when her mother told her she would cut out the size 9 tag signaling being larger was something to be ashamed of), and *actions matter* at all ages (children learn from observing, so if you're obsessed with thinness or your appearance, youngsters and those around you will think they should be too).

I'd like to think that if just one person reads *Flawless* and learns they don't have to look a certain way to be loved or valued - I think that's a win. If another reader decides to research diet culture or eating disorders on their own and stops looking down on themselves or others for their appearance, I think that's another win. If anyone else out there, like me, has finally decided to throw away their scale and reject diet culture to focus on their mental health and listening to their body to be the healthiest person they can be - it's another win.

Be kind to yourself.

And thank you...

The Selena Bailey series has been a passion project for me. I fell in love with Selena's character and the ability to bring awareness of real-world issues while entertaining. So I want to extend many thanks to all the people who have contributor to the series: my ARC team, my Betas and my editors (Dawn, Jon & Paula). I couldn't have brought Selena to life without all of you. And last, but not least, a huge thank you to my readers it's because of you that I continue to do what I love, writing stories.

H.K. Christie

THANK YOU!

Thank you for reading *Flawless*! I hope you enjoyed reading it as much as I loved writing it. If you did, I would greatly appreciate if you could post a short review.

Reviews are crucial for any author and can make a huge difference in visibility of current and future works. Reviews allow us to continue doing what we love, *writing stories*. Not to mention, I would be forever grateful!

Thank you!

ALSO BY H.K. CHRISTIE

The Martina Monroe Series is a nail-biting suspense series starring Private Investigator Martina Monroe. If you like high-stakes games, jaw-dropping twists, and embattled seekers struggling to do right, then you'll love H.K. Christie's thrilling series.

What She Left, Martina Monroe, PI, Book 1

She's on her last chance. When the bodies start piling up, she'll need to save more than her job.

Martina Monroe is a single bad day away from losing it all. Stuck catching insurance fraudsters and cheating spouses due to a DUI, the despondent PI yearns to return to more fulfilling gigs. So when a prospective client asks for her by name to identify an unknown infant in a family photo, she leaps at the opportunity and travels to the one place she swore never to go: back home.

As the pressure mounts and the temptation of booze calls like a siren, Martina digs into the mystery and discovers many of the threads have razor-sharp ends. And forced to partner with a resentful detective investigating a linked suspicious death, the haunted private eye unravels clues that delve deep into her past... and put her in a dark and dangerous corner.

Can this gritty detective unlock the truth before she's drowned in a sea of secrets?

What She Left is the page-turning first book in the Martina Monroe Private Investigator Series. If you like high-stakes games, jaw-dropping twists, and embattled seekers struggling to do right, then you'll love H.K. Christie's thrilling search for answers.

If She Ran, Martina Monroe, PI, Book 2

Three months. Three missing women. One PI determined to discover the truth.

Back from break, PI Martina Monroe clears the air with her boss at Drakos Security & Investigations and is ready to jump right into solving cold cases for the CoCo County Sheriff's Department.

Diving into the cold case files Martina stumbles upon a pattern of missing young women, all of whom were deemed runaways, and the files froze with minimal detective work from the original investigators. The more Martina digs into the women's last days the more shocking discoveries she makes.

Soon, Martina and Detective Hirsch not only uncover additional missing women but when their star witness turns up dead, they must rush to the next before it's too late.

A gripping, unputdownable thriller full of mystery and suspense.

All She Wanted, Martina Monroe, PI, Book 3

A tragic death. A massive cover-up. PI Martina Monroe must face her past in order to reveal the truth.

PI Martina Monroe has found her groove working cold cases alongside Detective Hirsch at the CoCo County Sheriff's Department. With a growing team of cold case detectives, Martina and Hirsch are on the heels of bringing justice for Julie DeSoto - a woman Martina failed to protect one year earlier. But when Martina receives a haunting request from her past, it nearly tears her in two.

As Julie's case turns hot, so does the investigation into a young soldier's untimely death. As both cases rattle Martina to the core, she now questions everything she believed about her time working for Drakos Security & Investigations and with the United States Army. Martina must uncover the truth for her sanity and her own life.

Pushed to the brink, Martina risks everything to expose the real criminals and bring justice for the victim's family and her own.

A gripping, page-turning thriller, full of suspense.

All She Wanted is the third installment in the thrilling Martina Monroe PI series.

The Selena Bailey Series is a suspenseful series featuring a young Selena Bailey and her turbulent path to becoming a top notch kickass private investigator as led by her mentor, Martina Monroe.

Not Like Her, Selena Bailey, Book 1

A battered mother. A possessive boyfriend. Can she save herself from a similar fate?

Selena longs to flee her uneasy home life. Prepping every spare minute for a college escape, the headstrong, high school senior vows never to be like her alcoholic mom with her string of abusive boyfriends. So when Selena finds her beaten nearly to death, she knows safety is slipping away...

With her mother's violent lover evading justice, Selena's new boyfriend's offer to move in seems Heaven-sent. But jealous rage and a renewed search for her long-lost father threaten to pull her back into harm's way.

Can Selena break free of an ugly past, or will brutal men crush her hopes of a better future?

Not Like Her is the first book in the suspenseful Selena Bailey series. If you like thrilling twists, dark tension, and smart and driven women, then you'll love H.K. Christie's new dark mystery series.

Trigger warning: This book includes themes relating to domestic violence

One In Five, Selena Bailey, Book 2

A predator running free and the girl determined to stop him.

After escaping a violent past, Selena Bailey, starts her first semester of college determined to put it all behind her - until her roommate is attacked at the Delta Kappa Alpha house. After reporting the attack, police refuse to prosecute due to lack of evidence, claiming another case of 'he said, she said'.

As Selena and Dee begin meeting other victims, it's clear Dee's assault wasn't an isolated event. Selena determined to take down the DKA house, takes matters into her own hands in order to claim justice for Dee and prevent the next attack.

Will Selena get justice for the women of SFU or will she become the next victim?

One In Five, is the second book in the suspenseful Selena Bailey series. If you like thrilling twists, dark tension, and smart and driven women, then you'll love H.K. Christie's dark mystery series.

On The Rise, Selena Bailey, Book 3

A little girl is taken. A mysterious cover-up. One young investigator determined to find the truth.

Selena Bailey, a sophomore at the local university studying criminal justice, returns from winter break to jump into her first official case as a private investigator with her stepmother's security firm.

Thrown into an undercover detail, Selena soon discovers a much darker plot. What seemed like a tragic kidnapping is revealed to be just the tip of the iceberg. Will Selena expose the truth before not only the little girl's life, but her own is lost forever?

On The Rise is the third standalone story in the suspenseful Selena Bailey series. If you like thrilling twists, dark tension, and smart and driven women, then you'll love H.K. Christie's new mystery series.

Go With Grace, Selena Bailey, Book 4

A dangerous stalker. A desperate classmate. Will one young investigator risk everything to help a stranger in need?

Selena Bailey returns in her senior year of college determined to keep her head down and out of other people's lives with the sole intent of keeping them safe and out of harm's way.

Selena is focused more than ever, with three major goals: graduate with her bachelor's degree in Criminal Justice, obtain her Private Investigator's license and find her late boyfriend, Brendon's, killers.

Her plans are derailed when a desperate classmate approaches Selena for her help. At first, she refuses but Dillon is certain his life is in danger and provides Selena with proof. With no one else to turn to, Selena reluctantly takes the case.

The investigation escalates quickly as Selena soon discovers the woman stalking Dillon is watching his, and now Selena's, every move.

Will Selena be able to save Dillon's life and her own?

Go With Grace is the fourth story, and first full-length novel, in the suspenseful Selena Bailey series. If you like thrilling twists, dark tension, and smart and driven women, then you'll love H.K. Christie's new thriller series.

Flawless, Selena Bailey, Book 5

A young woman clinging on to life. A desperate family

fighting for answers. Will Selena be able to discover the truth in time to save her?

Selena Bailey returns with her Private Investigator license in one hand and the first official case for Bailey Investigations in the other.

When the sister of a young woman, fighting for her life in the Intensive Care Unit, pleads with Selena to explore her sister, Stephanie's, last days before she slipped into a coma, Selena must go undercover in the billion dollar beauty industry to discover the truth.

The deeper Selena delves into Stephanie's world, the more she fears for Stephanie's life and so many others.

As Selena unravels the truth behind an experimental weight loss regimen, she finds it's not only weight the good doctor's patients are losing. Selena now must rush against the clock to save not only Stephanie's life, but her own.

Flawless is the fifth story, and 2nd full-length novel, in the suspenseful Selena Bailey series. If you like thrilling twists, dark tension, and smart and driven women, then you'll love H.K. Christie's new thriller series.

———

A Permanent Mark

A heartless killer. Weeks without answers. Can she move on when a murderer walks free?

Kendall Murphy's life comes crashing to a halt at the news her husband has been killed in a tragic hit-and-run. Devastated and out-of-sorts, she can't seem to come to terms with the senselessness of it all. Despite, promises by a young detective, she fears they'll never find the person responsible for her husband's death.

As months go by without answers, Kendall, with the help of her grandmother and sister, deals with her grief as she tries to create a new life for herself. But when the detective discovers that the death was a murder-for-hire, suddenly everyone from her new love interest and those closest to her are under suspicion. And it may only be a matter of time before the assassin strikes again...

Can Kendall trust anyone, or will misplaced loyalty make her the next victim?

If you like riveting suspense and gripping mysteries then you'll love *A Permanent Mark* - starring a grown up Selena Bailey.

Join the H.K. Christie Reader Club to be the first to hear about upcoming novels, new releases, giveaways, promotions, as well as, a **free e-copy of the Martina Monroe series prequel, *Crashing Down.***

It's completely free to sign up and you'll never be spammed by me, you can opt out easily at any time.

To sign up visit

www.authorhkchristie.com

and join today!

ABOUT THE AUTHOR

H.K. Christie is the author of suspenseful stories featuring unbreakable women.

When not working on her latest novel, she can be found eating, drinking, running slowly, or playing with her favorite furry pal. *Flawless* is her thirteenth novel.

She is a native and current resident of the San Francisco Bay Area.

www.authorhkchristie.com

Made in the USA
Coppell, TX
01 July 2022

79456557R00125